Midnight Prowlers

Other Collections by Phyllis R. Fenner

Behind the Wheel
Stories of Cars on Road and Track

Consider the Evidence
Stories of Mystery and Suspense

A Dog's Life
Stories of Champions, Hunters, and Faithful Friends

The Endless Dark
Stories of Underground Adventure

Full Forty Fathoms
Stories of Underwater Adventure

Gentle Like a Cyclone
Stories of Horses and Their Riders

Keeping Christmas
Stories of the Joyous Season

Lift Line
Stories of Downhill and Cross-Country Skiing

Perilous Ascent
Stories of Mountain Climbing

Where Speed Is King
Stories of Racing Adventure

Wide-Angle Lens
Stories of Time and Space

Midnight Prowlers

STORIES OF CATS
AND THEIR
ENSLAVED OWNERS

SELECTED BY

PHYLLIS R. FENNER

ILLUSTRATED BY GEORGE GERSHINOWITZ

William Morrow and Company
New York   1981

Grateful acknowledgment is made for permission to quote from the following:

"The Fat Cat" by Q. Patrick reprinted by permission of Curtis Brown, Ltd. Copyright 1945 by Q. Patrick.

"The Cat Who Lived in a Drainpipe" by Joan Aiken, from *The Faithless Lollybird* by Joan Aiken. Copyright © 1977 by Joan Aiken Enterprises Ltd. Reprinted by permission of Doubleday & Company, Inc. and Jonathan Cape, Ltd.

"The Cat" by Mary E. Wilkins Freeman reprinted from *Understudies* by Mary E. Wilkins Freeman.

"The Ginger King" by A. E. W. Mason reprinted by permission of Trinity College, Oxford, England.

"My Boss the Cat" by Paul Gallico reprinted by permission of Harold Ober Associates Incorporated. Copyright 1952 by the Crowell Collier Publishing Co., Inc. Renewed.

"The Luck of the Cat" by Elizabeth Goudge from *Pedlar's Pack* by Elizabeth Goudge. Reprinted by Books for Libraries Press. Distributed by Arno Press, Inc.

"Cat Nipped" from *The Collected Stories of Jack Schaefer*, published by Houghton Mifflin Company. Copyright © 1966 by Jack Schaefer. Reprinted by permission of the publisher.

"Total Loss" by Sylvia Townsend Warner reprinted by permission of the Estate of the author and Chatto & Windus Ltd.

"The Ninth Life" by Mazo de la Roche reprinted by permission of the Executors of the Estate of the author, Lang, Michener, Cranston, Farquharson & Wright.

"The Cyprian Cat" from *In the Teeth of the Evidence* by Dorothy L. Sayers. Copyright 1949 by Dorothy Leigh Sayers Fleming. Copyright renewed © 1967 by Anthony Fleming. Reprinted by permission of Harper & Row, Publishers, Inc.

Printed in the United States of America.
2   3   4   5   6   7   8   9   10

The Cataloging in Publication Data can be found opposite the Table of Contents.

For
Boots, Jennie, Suki, Betsy, Coco, Monroe,
and their enslaved owners.

Library of Congress Cataloging in Publication Data

Main entry under title:

Midnight prowlers.
  Summary: A collection of ten stories depicting cats in many guises.
  1. Cats—Legends and stories. 2. Children's stories, English. 3. Children's stories, American. [1. Cats—Fiction. 2. Short stories] I. Fenner, Phyllis R. (Phyllis Reid), 1899-
II. Gershinowitz, George.
PZ10.3.M5774 823'.01'0836 [Fic] 81-3953
ISBN 0-688-00704-X   AACR2
ISBN 0-688-00705-8 (lib. bdg.)

CONTENTS

CATS HERE,
CATS THERE,
CATS AND KITTENS
EVERYWHERE

Love cats or hate them, take them or leave them, everyone agrees they are mysterious. Cats are independent, temperamental, selfish, domineering, exasperating, and lovable. There is no tyranny so absolute—or so rewarding—as a cat's.

One's own cat is always exceptional. When you give it security, attention, and affection, it will respond with still another revelation of its intelligence. The personality of a cat is anything but monotonous.

The stories here are about all kinds of cats: tough alley cats, plain house cats, and supernatural cats. The range indicates some of the many different roles cats take on. No wonder they arouse such different emotions among human beings.

P.F.

The Fat Cat

Q. PATRICK

The marines found her when they finally captured the old mission house at Fufa. After two days of relentless pounding, they hadn't expected to find anything alive there—least of all a fat cat.

And she was a very fat cat, sandy as a Scotchman, with enormous agate eyes and a fat, amiable face. She sat there on the mat—or rather what was left of the mat—in front of what had been the mission porch, licking her paws as placidly as if the shell-blasted jungle were a summer lawn in New Jersey.

One of the men, remembering his childhood primer, quoted: "The fat cat sat on the mat."

The other men laughed; not that the remark was really funny, but laughter broke the tension and expressed their relief at having at last reached their objective, after two days of bitter fighting.

The fat cat, still sitting on the mat, smiled at them, as if to show she didn't mind the joke being on her. Then she saw Corporal Randy Jones and for some reason known only to herself ran toward him as though he were her long-lost master. With a refrigerator purr, she weaved in and out of his muddy legs.

Everyone laughed again as Randy picked her up and pushed his ugly face against the sleek fur. It was funny to see any living thing show a preference for the dour, solitary Randy.

A sergeant flicked his fingers. "Kitty. Come here. We'll make you B Company mascot."

But the cat, perched on Randy's shoulder like a queen on her throne, merely smiled down majestically as much as to say, "You can be my subjects if you like. But this is my man, my royal consort."

And never for a second did she swerve from her devotion. She lived with Randy, slept with him, ate only food provided by him. Almost every man in Company B tried to seduce her with caresses and morsels of canned ration, but all advances were met with a yawn of contempt.

For Randy this new love was ecstasy. He guarded her with the possessive tenderness of a mother. He combed her fur sleek; he almost starved himself to maintain her fatness. And all the time there was a strange wonder in him. The

The Fat Cat

homeliest and ungainliest of ten in a West Virginia mining family, he had never before aroused affection in man or woman. No one had counted for him until the fat cat.

Randy's felicity, however, was short-lived. In a few days B Company was selected to carry out a flanking movement to surprise and possibly capture the enemy's headquarters, known to be twenty miles away through dense, sniper-infested jungle. The going would be rugged. Each man would carry his own supply of food and water, and he would sleep in foxholes with no support from the base.

The C.O. was definite about the fat cat; the stricken Randy was informed that the presence of a cat would seriously endanger the safety of the whole company. If she were seen following him, she would be shot on sight. Just before their scheduled departure, Randy carried the fat cat over to the mess of Company H, where she was enthusiastically received by an equally fat cook. Randy could not bring himself to look back at the reproachful stare that he knew would be in the cat's agate eyes.

But all through that first day of perilous jungle travel, the thought of the cat's stare haunted him, and he was prey to all the heartache of parting; in leaving the cat, he had left behind wife, mother, and child.

Darkness, like an immense black parachute, had descended hours ago on the jungle, when Randy was awakened from exhausted sleep. Something soft and warm was brushing his cheek, and his foxhole resounded to a symphony of purring. He stretched out an incredulous hand, but this was no dream. Real and solid, the cat was curled in a contented ball at his shoulder.

His first rush of pleasure was chilled as he remembered his C.O.'s words. The cat, spurning the blandishments of H Company's cuisine, had followed him through miles of treacherous jungle, only to face death the moment daylight revealed her presence. Randy was in an agony of uncertainty. To carry her back to the base would be desertion. To beat and drive her away was beyond the power of his simple nature.

The cat nuzzled his face again and breathed a mournful meow. She was hungry, of course, after her desperate trek. Suddenly Randy saw what he must do. If he could bring himself not to feed her, hunger would surely drive her back to the sanctuary of the cook.

She meowed again. He shushed her and gave her a half-hearted slap. "Ain't got nothing for you, honey. Scram. Go home. Scat."

To his mingled pleasure and disappointment, she leaped silently out of the foxhole. When morning came, there was no sign of her.

As B Company inched its furtive advance through the dense undergrowth, Randy felt the visit from the cat must have been a dream. But on the third night she came again. She brushed against his cheek and daintily took his ear in her teeth. When she meowed, the sound was still soft and cautious, but held a pitiful quaver of beseechment, which cut through Randy like a bayonet.

On her first visit, Randy had not seen the cat, but tonight some impulse made him reach for his flashlight. Holding it carefully downward, he turned it on. What he saw was the ultimate ordeal. The fat cat was fat no longer. Her body sagged; her sleek fur was matted and mud-stained, her paws torn and bloody. But it was the eyes, blinking up at him, that were the worst. There was no hint of reproach in them, only an expression of infinite trust and pleading.

Forgetting everything but those eyes, Randy tugged out one of his few remaining cans of ration. At the sight of it, the cat weakly licked its lips. Randy moved to open the can. Then the realization that he would be signing the cat's death warrant surged over him. And, because his pent-up emotion had to have some outlet, it turned into unreasoning anger against this animal whose suffering had become more than he could bear. "Skat," he hissed. But the cat did not move.

He lashed out at her with the heavy flashlight. For a second she lay motionless under the blow. Then with a little moan she fled.

The next night she did not come back and Randy did not sleep.

On the fifth day they reached really dangerous territory. Randy and another marine, Joe, were sent forward to scout for the Japanese command headquarters. Suddenly, weaving through the jungle, they came upon it.

A profound silence hung over the glade, with its two hastily erected shacks. Peering through dense foliage, they saw traces of recent evacuation—waste paper scattered on the grass, a pile of fresh garbage, a Japanese Army shirt flapping on a tree. Outside one of the shacks, under an awning, stretched a rough table strewn with the remains of a meal. "They must have got wind of us and scrammed," breathed Joe.

Randy edged forward, then froze as something stirred in the long grasses near the door of the first shack. As he watched, the once fat cat hobbled out into the sunlight.

A sense of heightened danger warred with Randy's pride that she had not abandoned him. Stiff with suspense, he watched her disappear into the shack. Soon she padded out.

"No Japs," said Joe. "That cat'd have raised 'em sure as shooting."

He started boldly into the glade. "Hey, Randy, there's a whole chicken on that table. Chicken's going to taste good after K ration."

He broke off, for the cat had seen the chicken too, and with pitiful clumsiness had leaped onto the table. With an angry yell Joe stooped for a rock and threw it.

Indignation blazed in Randy. He'd starved and spurned the cat, and yet she'd followed him with blind devotion. The chicken, surely, should be her reward. In his slow, simple mind it seemed the most important thing in the world for his beloved to have her fair share of the booty.

The cat, seeing the rock coming, lumbered off the table just in time, for the rock struck the chicken squarely, knocking it off its plate.

Randy leaped into the clearing. As he did so, a deafening explosion made him drop to the ground. A few seconds later, when he raised himself, there was no table, no shack, nothing but a blazing wreckage of wood.

Dazedly he heard Joe's voice. "Booby trap under that chicken. Gee, if that cat hadn't jumped for it, I wouldn't have hurled the rock; we'd have grabbed it ourselves, and we'd be in heaven now." His voice dropped to an awed whisper. "That cat. I guess it's blown to hell. . . . But it saved our lives." Randy couldn't speak. There was a constriction in his throat. He lay there, feeling more desolate than he'd ever felt in his life before.

Then from behind came a contented purr.

He spun round. Freakishly the explosion had hurled a crude rush mat out of the shack. It had come to rest on the grass behind him.

And, seated serenely on the mat, the cat was smiling at him.

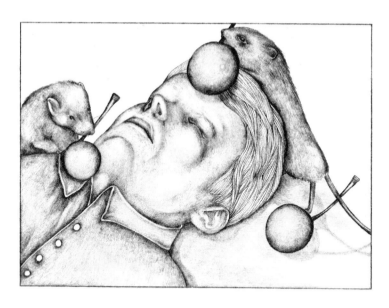

The Cat Who Lived in a Drainpipe

JOAN AIKEN

Three hundred years ago, in the times when men wore swords and rode on horses, when ladies carried fans and traveled in carriages, when ships had sails and kings lived in castles, and you could buy a large loaf of bread for a penny, there lived three cats in Venice.

Venice is a very peculiar town, built on about a hundred islands. The streets in between the houses are canals full of water. Only in the narrowest alleys and lanes can you

The Cat Who Lived in a Drainpipe

walk on dry ground. If you want to go across town you take a gondola. If a housewife wants to visit her neighbor on the other side of the street, she has to row herself over, unless there is a bridge by her house. Children and cats in Venice learn to swim almost as soon as they learn to walk.

The three cats I am going to tell you about were called Nero, Sandro, and Seppi.

Nero was large and pitch-black and very tough indeed. His master was a chimney sweep called Benno Fosco. Nero helped with the sweeping. In Venice, chimneys are swept from above. The sweep, standing on the roof, lets down a long bunch of twigs like a witch's broom to knock out the soot. Nero and his master climbed all over the roofs of Venice with their brooms and their bags full of soot. If a chimney was narrow or very choked up, Nero would go down first, at top speed, like a diver, boring out the soot with his sharp claws and his powerful paws and sweeping it loose behind him with his strong, whiplike tail.

It was lucky that Nero was black, so that the soot didn't show on his fur; he was always absolutely wadded with soot and left a cloud of it behind him as he walked about. And if his master rubbed behind his ears, out came another black cloud. No one, apart from Benno Fosco, would ever have dared to stroke Nero; he might have bitten the finger off anybody who tried. When the chimney sweep poled his gondola along the canals, loaded with sacks of soot, Nero sat on one of the bags, right at the front, looking like a big fat figurehead carved out of coal. Mostly he stayed silent, but every once in a while he let out a single low, threatening howl: *Ow-wow-ow-ow-ow!* It meant, Does anybody feel like a fight? And when he did so, the other

19

cats along the waterside, sitting on windowsills or door-steps or on bridges or other boats, would half close their eyes, shrug, and keep quite quiet until he had gone by. Nobody ever felt inclined to fight with Nero.

Sandro was quite a different kind of cat. His long, soft fur was a dark orange color, like a French marigold. His expression was always calm and sleepy and very refined; he spent most of his days dozing on a red velvet cushion in the boudoir of his mistress, who was a princess and lived in a palace in one of the grandest streets. Two or three times a day, the princess used to comb Sandro with a silver comb. While doing so she would exclaim admiringly, "*Bello* Sandro! *Bello gatto!* Beautiful cat!" Sandro never paid the least attention to this, but merely went on dozing harder than ever, with his nose pushed well in under his tail. The only exercise he took during the hours of daylight was an occasional short spell of washing. But at night, when his mistress, the Princess Cappella, was asleep, he went out over the roofs of Venice.

Seppi, the third cat, was quite different again from either of the others. For a start, he was much smaller. Seppi belonged to nobody; he had been born in a worm-eaten fish basket, and he lived in a broken drainpipe. His mother, unfortunately, had fallen off a fishing boat and been drowned when he was a kitten; from that day on, Seppi never grew any bigger. He lived on fish heads and moldy scraps of macaroni stolen from garbage heaps. He was an ugly little cat, black and white in patches of various sizes, with one black paw and three white, a black mask across his white face, and a saddle of black from shoulders to tail. One ear was black with a white lining, and one white with a black tip; one eye was yellow, and one blue. Also, he had suffered from a mishap to his tail; most of it was missing, leaving only a short black stump. It made him look like a rabbit and ruined his balance. Where other cats could leap gracefully onto narrow ledges or walk easily along slender rails, Seppi had to concentrate with all his might or he was liable to overshoot and topple off edges. But he practiced at balancing most patiently, and when he did fall he always landed lightly; he was so skinny that he weighed little more than a duster. Every day he clambered gaily and dangerously all over the roofs and walls and pinnacles and boats and bridges of Venice; he was always hungry but he was always hopeful, too, and full of energy and curiosity. People laughed at him and shouted *"Pulcinello"* as he went trotting by on his own business, because, in his black mask, he looked so like a clown.

These three cats, Nero, Sandro, and Seppi, were not precisely friends. Nero was too tough to need friends, and Sandro too lazy. And both were inclined to look down their noses at Seppi, who was such a common little gutter cat and so much younger and smaller as well.

But one bond joined all three of them together, and that was music. They were all passionately fond of it. Regularly, every Friday evening, they assembled together for a singing session. They always met in the same place, on a wooden humpbacked bridge over a quiet backwater. And there, all night, in all weather except snow, they would hold their concert, until the first light of the rising sun began to dapple the canal water like pink lettuce leaves.

This was why Nero and Sandro were prepared to tolerate Seppi and overlook his clownlike appearance and vulgar ways and lack of tail. In spite of his being so small, he had a remarkably loud voice, and furthermore he could sing higher up the scale than any other cat in Venice.

Their program of singing was always the same. Nero began, because his voice was the deepest. Squatting on the top step of the bridge, like a big shapeless black lump, with elbows and whiskers sticking out sideways, he would slowly let out four or five howls, all on the same deep, gritty, throbbing bass note, like an old millwheel creaking: *How, row, row, row, row.*

Then there would be a long, silent pause, until Sandro was ready to sing his part of the trio, which was a slow, sorrowful, wailing tenor cry, not unlike the hoot of a ship's siren a great way off in the fog: *Harayyyyyyyyyyyyyy?*

Afterward, all three cats would sit silent and motionless, without even the twitch of a whisker, for so great a stretch of time that any listener might be fooled into thinking that they had finished their concert and gone home to bed. But not a bit of it. All of a sudden little Seppi would let out such an ear-piercingly shrill scream—*Freeeeeeeeeeeee!*—that birds, even at dead of night, would wake and twitter in protest under the eaves of nearby houses, dogs would bark for two miles around, while any person walking rather close to a canal in that district would almost certainly be so startled that he fell into the water. Even Sandro and Nero never became completely accustomed to Seppi's shriek; each time, after he had sung his part, they would gaze at him almost respectfully for a few moments.

Then they would repeat the recital, always in the same order, with Nero singing first and Seppi coming in at the end, and long pauses in between the solo parts. At the very

end, there would be a short chorus, with all singing together.

Very occasionally, a strange cat might make an attempt
to join their group, but neither Sandro nor Nero would
dream of permitting this. Sandro would let out a terrifying
hiss, and Nero would shoot from his place on the top step
and give the impertinent candidate such a clip on the ear
with a sooty paw that he would fly for his life and think
himself lucky to escape with his ears and tail.

In this way, the concerts were held every Friday night.
Half the cats of Venice came to listen and sat in admiring
silence, at a respectful distance.

Then, at sunrise, the three singers would silently part
and go their various ways: Nero flitting over the rooftops
to the first job of the day; Seppi trotting off through a network of narrow lanes and alleys, where he might hope to
find a fish tail or a couple of inches of cast-off spaghetti;
Sandro gracefully waving his golden tail and summoning
a boat to take him back to the palace where he lived. All
the gondoliers who plied their boats for hire along the
Venetian canals knew the Princess Cappella and her cat;
Sandro never had the least trouble in finding a gondola to
take him home. Any boatman who picked him up knew
that a fee of three golden ducats would be paid without
question by the butler who opened the door.

So matters went on for many months.

But one Friday evening in a cold November, when
Sandro and Nero reached the bridge at their usual hour,
they were surprised to see that Seppi was not there. Usually he was first at the meeting place, having nothing to
do apart from hunting for scraps in the gutters, whereas

Nero might be kept late sweeping a chimney, and Sandro might have been obliged to accompany his mistress on a round of calls.

"Where can the little wretch have got to?" Sandro said impatiently, after they had waited for ten minutes. He shivered, for an icy wind was blowing. "I wish he'd hurry up. There's nothing to beat music for warming you."

"Shall we start without him?" suggested Nero.

"No, it would be hopeless without the treble part. I do trust the little fool hasn't been kicked into a canal and drowned."

"More likely got into a fight with someone bigger than himself and had his head bitten off," said Nero uneasily. "Now I come to think about it, I haven't seen him around the streets for the last few days."

"No, it's all right. Here he comes," said Sandro in relief, noticing a small black-and-white shape slip along the top of a wall.

Seppi trotted up the steps to join his fellow singers. But he did not seem quite his usual, carefree self. He offered no explanation as to why he was late, he made no apologies, even when Nero growled at him and Sandro let out a reproving hiss, but sat in silence, with his feet apart and mouth open, staring up dreamily and absentmindedly at the small, frozen-looking moon that floated overhead. Furthermore, when it came to his turn to sing, he waited so long that both his companions began to wonder anxiously if he had lost his voice. And when he did at last let out his screech, it was nothing like so loud and shattering as usual; in fact, it was quite a soft, plaintive note, not much louder than the cry of a gull, and both Nero and Sandro were quite disgusted by it.

"Come on, sing up, you good-for-nothing!" said Nero, giving him a box on the ear. "What kind of a noise is *that?* A newborn kitten would be better. Why, a person could hardly hear it across the canal."

"Are you sick?" inquired Sandro, more sympathetically.

"No, no," murmured Seppi in a vague manner, still staring at the moon.

"Well, then, kindly pull yourself together!" said Nero sharply.

Afterward, Seppi did pull himself together and sang even better than usual, so well, in fact, that dogs barked all the way to the village of Mestre, and the other two forgot his strange behavior.

But, next week, they had cause to remember it again, for he arrived even later than on the previous Friday and in a most peculiar state, with his whiskers dangling downward, faraway eyes narrowed to slits, and a layer of dust and cobwebs all over his fur.

Moreover, when it came to his turn to sing, all he could let out was a faint squeak, hardly louder than the noise made by a bat.

"Look here, this is useless!" said Nero in disgust. "Come on, you'll have to tell us what's up. Where have you been all week? I haven't seen you since last Friday. Where are you spending your time these days?"

"Yes, speak up, Seppi," added Sandro. "You owe it to us to tell us what's happened. After all, we taught you all the music you know."

At that, Seppi was suddenly galvanized; his faraway look vanished, his stump of a tail and scanty whiskers bristled, and he burst into speech.

"Music?" he said. "Oh, my dear partners, you think we

are producing good music here? You think our trio makes the best music in Venice? Just come with me. I'll take you where you can hear something that will make you realize we don't know the first thing about music!"

At this, Nero and Sandro exchanged glances. The little fellow must have gone crazy, their eyes and ears and whiskers suggested. Sandro elegantly shrugged his tail. Oh, well, we'll have to humor him. Perhaps we can get him out of this nonsensical fit somehow. Otherwise, we'd better start looking for another treble. Too bad.

Anyway, they followed him.

Seppi bolted down the balustrade of the bridge and along the path beside the canal. Then he led the way at a gallop through twisting alleys, across paved squares, over bridges, along quaysides, until they had come to a much grander and richer part of the town.

Here Seppi went upward—up onto a gate, along a wall, onto a roof, and from there in a long leap across an alley onto a higher roof.

"Why are you bringing us here?" said Nero. "I know this house. It belongs to a wealthy paper manufacturer. I've often swept the chimneys. Once the mistress gave me a whole bowlful of fresh sardines."

"Yes, yes, I daresay. Come along," said Seppi inattentively, and he led them up and up, toward an attic window. "Now come up here and keep quiet and listen!"

The window was a kind of dormer, right in the middle of the roof. All three cats perched on the sill, which was very dusty. It was only a few feet above the level of the flat roof (which was lucky, for Seppi was in such an excited state that he kept losing his balance and toppling off the edge). "Now listen, listen!" he begged again, breath-lessly.

Nero and Sandro peered through the window, to see what had made their young colleague so excited. They were looking down into a smallish attic containing nothing save a chair, a box, and a music stand. On the box lay an oboe. On the chair sat a young man, who was tuning a violin, and a minute or two after they had settled on the sill he began to play it.

As he played, Nero's and Sandro's eyes became larger and larger, rounder and rounder. Presently Nero surrep-titiously wiped a tear off his black nose with the back of his paw. Sandro was soon so overcome by emotion that he had to bury his face in his bushy, golden tail. As for Seppi, his blue eye and his yellow one were shining like a sapphire and a topaz respectively.

"There!" he whispered during a pause. "Did you ever hear anything as beautiful as that? Ever in your *life?*"

Speechlessly they shook their heads. They were quite choked with wonder and awe, both at the skill of the player and the magic of the music.

"There!" said Seppi again, when the player had finished his piece. "What did I tell you? Now do you see why I have been a bit absentminded lately? I've spent the whole of every day just sitting on this windowsill, listening to him play."

"Who is the young man?" inquired Sandro graciously, when he had recovered himself a little.

"I know him," said Nero. "He is the paper manufac-turer's son. His name is Tomaso. Once, when I had gone down the chimney and come out into a big saloon downstairs, I heard his father say to him, 'Tomaso, my son, music is a fine thing, but why don't you ever go out and amuse yourself like the other young men? Why spend all your days playing your fiddle up there in the attic?' And the mother said to her husband, 'Oh, leave the boy alone, Antonio! If he wants to play his fiddle and his oboe, that's a harmless hobby for a young man, and not at all expensive.' "

Now the young man began to play again, on the oboe this time, and the tunes he played were so supremely beautiful that Sandro was soon heaving with silent sobs, thinking of his childhood, while Nero had to run twice around the dormer to recover himself. Both of them thanked Seppi from the bottom of their hearts for having given them such a musical treat.

From that time on, there were no more concerts on the bridge. Not Friday night only, but every evening of the week was spent by the three partners perched on the dusty sill, listening wide-eyed and openmouthed to the music made by young Tomaso in his attic. Their own music making was entirely abandoned; all the cats in Venice wondered what had become of the famous trio and grieved at their loss. Indeed, another trio of cats had the impudence to take over the wooden bridge, but their singing was so inferior that the whole audience joined together to chase them off, and from that time on Friday nights in that quarter were no different from any other. The people in the houses round about were not sorry, but the cat population thought it a sad loss.

During daylight, of course, Nero and Sandro were obliged to return to their usual occupations, which they did most reluctantly. Benno Fosco soon began to grumble that Nero's chimney sweeping was becoming very hasty and careless; the Princess Cappella complained that her pet's fur was disgracefully dusty and neglected; little Seppi gave such scanty attention to hunting for scraps of food that he grew as thin as a withered leaf. He stayed on the windowsill all day long unless young Tomaso went out for a short airing. When he did so, Seppi would hastily scramble down from the roof and try to follow him, either slipping along behind through the lanes and squares or nipping on board his gondola, where, perched in some cranny, he would watch the young man with unblinking love and admiration.

Oh, he often thought sadly to himself, how happy I would be if only I could belong to him, as Sandro does to the princess. How proud I would be to sit on the prow of his boat as it glided along the canal. Or he would imagine lying on a blue velvet cushion in a warm room, listening to his master play for hours. Surely life could hold no greater happiness than that.

Still, he thought, I might as well put such ideas out of my head. He could have the handsomest cat in Venice. He'd never look at an ugly little cat like me.

In fact, once or twice, young Tomaso had noticed Seppi stowed in a corner of his gondola and had called to the gondolier, "Is that cat yours?"

"No, sir, that's little Seppi. He belongs nowhere. He's nobody's cat."

"How did he get on board?"

The boatman would shrug.

"Well, throw him off; he's probably full of fleas!"

Seppi was quite resigned to being thrown off the boat if discovered and would simply return to the attic window-sill and wait for Tomaso to come back.

Due to this habit of following the young man and listening to his conversation, Seppi was better informed about the family's affairs than the other two partners.

Two or three months later, there came a violent quarrel between Tomaso and his father, which ended in the young man's rushing up to the attic and slamming the door. The father hardly ever climbed above the first floor, where the grand reception rooms were, but on this occasion he came storming up after his son.

"If that's your last word," he shouted through the door, "you can just stay in the attic till you change your mind." And he locked the door and pocketed the key.

Tomaso made no reply.

"I shall tell the servants not to let you have any food or drink until you get this ridiculous notion out of your head!" shouted old Antonio furiously.

Tomaso answered nothing.

"And you needn't think you can talk your mother around, for I'm taking her off to stay with Auntie Gabriella in the country!" roared the old man, and he stamped away downstairs.

"What's all that about?" said Sandro to Seppi (for it was evening, and all three cats were there). "What has young Tomaso done that's so upset the old man?"

"He has fallen in love with a girl at one of the orphanages. He wants to marry her."

(There were four big orphanages in Venice, where the orphans were all taught music and learned to sing most beautifully.)

The Cat Who Lived in a Drainpipe

"*Dio mio!*" said Nero. "What possessed him to do that? I thought the orphans were all bowlegged or one-eyed."

"Not this one," said Seppi. "I've seen Tomaso meet her. She is very pretty. And she has a fine singing voice. Her name is Margherita."

"Then why won't his father let Tomaso marry her?"

"He wants his son to marry some rich girl."

"Humph," said Sandro. "I daresay Tomaso will give in when he begins to feel really hungry."

"If he had any gumption he'd escape over the roof," said Nero.

"He could never do it," said Seppi. "A cat could, but not a human being."

It was true that the house was extremely high; the roof commanded a beautiful view over half of Venice, but there was no way down, except for cats. Next morning young Tomaso found that out for himself; he climbed out his window, walked around the roof inspecting its possibilities, and then, shrugging, returned to the attic, where he spent the day composing and playing the most heart-rending tunes.

"The parents have gone off to the country," reported Seppi, when Sandro and Nero arrived that evening. "And they took all the servants with them except for a very bad-tempered steward, who has orders not to allow Tomaso any food until he writes a letter to his father promising to stop thinking about the girl."

Indeed, at that moment, they heard the steward, whose name was Michele, banging on the attic door. "Will you write to your father and say you have changed your mind?"

"Never!" shouted the young man, and he blew a defiant blast on his oboe.

31

"Then you get no supper," said Michele, and they heard his footsteps retreating down the stairs.

Two days went by.

"This is becoming serious," said Sandro. "The young man is growing pale and thin. Human beings have to eat a lot in order to survive. Suppose he should die? No more music!"

Even Nero looked grave, and little Seppi nearly fell off the windowsill at such a dreadful idea. During the next day, with terrible difficulty because of his poor balance, he lugged up two large fish heads onto the roof and laid them hopefully on the windowsill. But the prisoner inside did not seem to notice them. After another night, Tomaso just lay all day on his cloak, which was spread on the floor; he seemed to be very weak and did not play on his violin, though he occasionally blew a few notes on his oboe.

"A terrible thing has happened!" reported Seppi agitatedly, when Sandro and Nero arrived on the following evening.

"What now?"

"That steward, Michele, he got mixed up in a fight with some sailors on the quayside. I was watching from the garden wall. A stone hit him on the head, and he was carried off as if he were dead."

"So now nobody in Venice knows that the poor young man is starving in the attic?" said Sandro.

"*Zio mio!* That's bad," said Nero.

"It's up to us to do something about him," said Seppi.

"But what?" said Sandro.

All three sat racking their brains.

"He needs food," said Nero, after a lot of thought.

"He didn't see the fish heads I brought him," said Seppi sadly.

"Fish heads are no use," said Sandro with scorn. "Human beings don't eat that kind of stuff."

There was another long, worried silence.

"If only we could get through the window," said Seppi. But it was shut tight. All their poking and prying had no effect. And the young man was lying with his back to them, without moving, as if he were very weak indeed.

At last Seppi said, looking rather embarrassed, "I think I have had an idea."

"Well, what is it?" said Nero. "Come on, speak up."

"Well," Seppi said, more and more bashful as the other two waited expectantly, "I have a—a sort of a friend; he—he occupies the other end of the drainpipe where I live."

"Who is this person?"

Nero and Sandro exchanged looks and shrugs. Evidently it was some frightfully low connection, though what alley cat could be lower down the social scale than Seppi, it was hard to imagine.

"His name is Umberto," muttered Seppi, blushing under his fur.

"Never heard of him. I thought I knew all the cats in Venice," said Nero.

"Umberto isn't—isn't exactly a cat."

"Well? What is he?"

"He's—he's a—a m-mouse."

"What!" Nero and Sandro nearly fell off the sill in their outrage and disapproval.

"A highly intelligent mouse, of course," Seppi went on hastily, gabbling in his anxiety. "He saved my life once, when I had a fishbone stuck in my throat. He pulled it out."

"Well?" demanded Nero after another awful silence. "What is your idea in regard to this *mouse*?"

"Don't you see?" Seppi picked up courage a little. "Mice can get *into* places. If I brought Umberto here—but you would have to promise to—to respect his advisory position —he could probably nibble a way into the attic. And he could carry in food."

"What sort of food could *he* take?" said Sandro scornfully.

Seppi had been thinking hard about this.

"Well, cheese. Peas. Things that a mouse can carry."

"Humph," said Nero. "Yes. It's a possibility, I will admit. Anyway, there's no use discussing what he could carry until we have met this character and he has surveyed the situation. Could you fetch him here, Seppi?"

"I could try."

"Trying is not good enough. I had better come with you," said Sandro. "You have such a wretched sense of balance; it would be disastrous if you dropped this person on your way here. I'm sure he's the only mouse in Venice who has ever got into conversation with a cat."

"All right, come along if you think so," agreed Seppi doubtfully. "But you will be careful with him, won't you?"

"Honor of a Cappella. I've often carried out the kitchen cat's kittens when they get into my mistress's boudoir. I know all about handling."

Seppi was so worried about Tomaso that he wasn't particularly embarrassed at taking Sandro to his humble home. His mind was occupied with the problem of what food could be transported to the attic. Eggs? Could mice carry eggs? Carrots? Meatballs?

Umberto was a large, stocky brown mouse with flashing black eyes and a gray muzzle, whiskers, and tail, for he was fairly advanced in years. Seppi had already told him about the poor young man's plight, so he was not greatly astonished when the two cats arrived at his end of the drainpipe and asked if he would come with them, though he did not look altogether happy at the prospect of being carried there in Sandro's mouth.

However, Sandro proved to be a careful and reliable bearer; in record time he carried Umberto back over the walls and rooftops as delicately as if he had had a peacock's egg between his jaws. Umberto certainly had a more comfortable ride than he would have if Seppi had carried him by the scruff of his neck, though Seppi did wonder, when they arrived at the attic windowsill, if Umberto's whiskers had not gone a shade or two whiter.

Nevertheless, the minute he was set down, the mouse began to bustle about the windowsill, surveying its possibilities in a thoroughly professional manner.

"Why, this will be quite easy," he said. "In fact, there is already a mousehole through the wooden window frame; it has been blocked with putty and scraps of paper, but I can clear that out in fifteen minutes."

And he began briskly nibbling with his razor-sharp teeth and scooping out the debris with his tiny but strong and skillful paws.

The other three sat watching and wishing they could do something helpful.

"Why don't you fetch some food while I do this?" Umberto suggested, when he came out of his tunnel for a mouthful of fresh air.

This seemed a good idea. Sandro and Nero left at once. But Seppi said that he would remain behind and help.

"When you have made the hole just a little bigger, I can poke in my paw and bring out the loose stuff."

In ten minutes Nero and Sandro returned, Nero with a hunk of parmesan cheese, Sandro carrying half a long, thin loaf of bread. They had stolen these things from a *trattoria* at the end of the street.

"Excellent," said Umberto, who was gaining more confidence as he became used to the situation. "Now if Seppi can push in his paw once more, I think it will be possible to push the rest of the barrier through into the attic."

Seppi thrust his paw in up to the shoulder and managed to shift the rest of the stopping; then Umberto ran through the tunnel.

"All clear," he reported, coming back. "And the young man is asleep, not dead; he's breathing, but his eyes are shut."

Meanwhile, the others had been nibbling off small scraps of cheese and bread of a suitable size to be taken in through the hole. Umberto carried some of them in and laid them beside the young man. His report was unpromising, however.

"He doesn't seem to want to wake up and eat them. Human beings are so sluggish! If you put delicious, strong-smelling cheese beside a sleeping mouse, he would be awake in a moment."

"Could you lay a crumb or two on his mouth?" suggested Seppi.

The Cat Who Lived in a Drainpipe

Umberto tried.

"No good," he came back to say presently. "The young man just brushes them off with his hand. And his head is as hot as a fire. I think he has a fever."

"When my mistress had a fever," said Sandro, "she ate a lot of fruit. Oranges and melons."

"Melons! How are we going to carry *melons* up here?" said Nero irritably.

"I have an idea!" said Seppi. "Grapes! And I know where there are some, too. Down below, at the back of this house, there is a big glass room—sometimes I come up that way over its roof—and inside there is a vine covered with grapes. Umberto, couldn't you go down inside the house and fetch some, or ask the house mice to help? There must be plenty inside somewhere. Every house in Venice is full of mice."

"I will see if it can be done," said Umberto. And he disappeared back through the tunnel. Presently he pushed his head out to announce that it was possible to squeeze under the attic door and he intended to go on a journey of exploration. He vanished again and did not return for a long time.

By now the night was nearly past. Roosters were crowing in backyards, and all the domes and pinnacles of Venice were beginning to turn pink. Nero and Sandro reluctantly went off to their day's duties.

"But we'll come back this evening," they promised.

"Bring some food when you come," begged Seppi. "Or some drink."

"*Drink!* How do you expect us to do that?"

But then Nero reflected. "My master has a leather wine

bottle that's not too big. I might be able to carry it. But how shall we get it into the attic? It's far too large to go through that hole."

"Perhaps Umberto can make the hole bigger before you come back. Or I can. I'll work at it all day."

After they had gone, Seppi turned to a plan of his own. Umberto's opening of the passage had slightly loosened the bottom left-hand windowpane. Seppi pushed his paw into the mousehole and worked it from side to side, shoving with his shoulder against the loose pane, which rattled and shifted and gave, little by little. But it was slow, hard, tiring work; he wished that Umberto would come back and help by nibbling away the putty around the edge of the pane. Seppi tried to do this himself, but his teeth were not the right shape. He went back to pushing and poking. After a couple more hours of this—all of a sudden, triumph! —the pane fell inward, onto the floor, with a tinkling crash.

It was a very small pane, however. Seppi wondered if he would be able to squeeze through the square hole that it had left. I shall look a real fool if I get stuck halfway, he thought, and tried his whiskers for size. They fitted exactly. Holding his breath, Seppi wriggled through. He could just do so, due to his extra thinness from the past few days of anxiety.

At last he was in the attic, where he had so often longed to be! It's lucky I'm small, he reflected; neither Nero nor Sandro could have done it.

He crept across the floor to where Tomaso lay on the cloak and sniffed the young man all over. Alive, thank goodness! But Umberto was right; Tomaso was certainly sick. His hands and forehead were burning hot, his lips were dry and cracked, and he tossed from side to side, muttering in his feverish dream: "*Mamma!* Please don't punish me. I played that last piece too fast, I must play it again slower. Margherita, why won't you come to see me? Please look this way—"

Seppi was greatly distressed at being able to do so little for his hero. He licked Tomaso's forehead all over several times, in hopes of cooling it a little; he fetched in some more of the bread and cheese from outside. But it was plain that the young man was too seriously ill to benefit from this kind of food.

At last, to his great relief, Seppi heard a soft snuffling and scraping from the other side of the attic door and turned in time to see Umberto squeeze underneath, rolling in front of him a large green grape. He was followed by a second mouse—a third—a fourth—a fifth. Each of them had brought a grape. More and more mice came pouring in, until the attic floor was quite covered with mice, and grapes were rolling about everywhere.

"Oh, *bravo, bravo!* Well done, my dear, dear friend!" exclaimed Seppi joyfully. "Now if only we can get the young man to eat one of the grapes—"

Easier said than done, however. Seppi tried dropping the grapes onto Tomaso's mouth. But, like the bread and cheese crumbs, they only rolled off. "And, in any case, he might choke if one went into his throat," pointed out Umberto. "Like you with the fishbone, Seppi."

At last they solved the problem. Working together, two of the mice, one seated on Tomaso's collar and one on his cheekbone, managed to squeeze a grape so that its juice ran into the corner of the patient's open mouth.

"He swallowed!" cried Seppi. "I saw his throat move. Quickly! Another grape!"

In no time they had a relay system working. Grapes were passed from paw to paw, as fast as drops of rain running down a railing. When, fairly soon, the two grape squeezers became exhausted, with aching paws and heaving chests, they were replaced by two others. Mice rushed to and fro, under the door, down the stairs to the hothouse, where the vine grew. The patient swallowed and swallowed, always with his eyes shut.

Finally he gave a deep sigh and shut his mouth tight, so that the juice from the last grape ran over his chin. Then he turned over, burying his face in his folded arm; two of the mouse squeezers narrowly avoided being squashed.

"I think he has had enough for now," said Umberto. "Sick people should not have much at a time. But I believe the grapes have done good."

It was true that the young man was breathing more easily. His head was not so hot, and he had stopped talking in his sleep. The mice ran all over him sympathetically.

"*Poverino!* Poor young man. It is a shame. His parents should not treat him so. Such a handsome young fellow, too!"

"I expect they did not mean him to die," Seppi said. "They believe the steward is here to keep an eye on him."

"But he is not! He has never come back. Downstairs the house is quite empty."

"Is there any food about?"

"Some. Not a lot. What should we bring up?"

"Anything you can carry."

So, during the rest of the day, there was a continuous

come-and-go of mice, up and down the stairs, and under the attic door, with all the food they could find and carry: nuts, olive, dried cherries, beans, Brussels sprouts, grains of rice, more grapes, small pieces of carrot, of artichoke, of cheese, of dried fish.

Seppi sat by the young man, lovingly licking and relicking his forehead all day, over and over, until his tongue became quite tired and dry. Twice more Tomaso half woke and was given more grape juice each time by relays of helpful mice.

After dark, Nero and Sandro returned. They were staggering with fatigue. Between them, taking it in turns, they had carried up a heavy leather bottle.

"*Dio mio!*" Nero said. "It will be days before my neck muscles recover from carrying that thing. But I think we can just squeeze it through the hole. What a lucky thing that you managed to get that pane out."

Nero and Sandro pushed; Seppi gripped the neck of the flask and pulled. At last it fell through onto the floor.

"What's in it? Wine?"

"No, much better," said Sandro. "*Teriaca!* My mistress got it from a witch."

Teriaca was a kind of medicine much used in Venice at that time. It was made from cinnamon, pepper, fennel, rose leaves, amber, gum arabic, opium, and many other herbs and spices. It was supposed to cure everything except the plague.

"How are we going to get the cork out?"

The mice were equal to that. They soon had the cork nibbled away.

Now came a difficulty, though. Even Seppi and the mice

41

together were not strong enough to hoist up the bottle to Tomaso's mouth, and there was a great danger, as they pushed and pulled, that all the precious contents would be spilled. Nero and Sandro, watching through the window, shouted advice but couldn't get in to help; the hole was too small for either of them to climb through. "Prop his head on the violin. No, on the oboe!" But this proved impossible.

"Well, we'll have to use drastic measures," Seppi announced, and, ordering the mice to keep the bottle tipped upward as close to the young man's face as possible, he bit Tomaso's hand sharply.

Roused by the sudden pain, the young man opened his eyes and saw the bottle right in front of them.

"I'm dreaming, dreaming," he murmured, but he raised himself on one elbow, grasped the bottle, and drank off its powerful-smelling contents in one long swallow. Then he fell back again and shut his eyes.

"*Bravo, bravo!*" cried the mice. "Now he will be better! The *teriaca* will cure him! All we need do is keep him fed, and soon we shall be hearing his beautiful music again.

"And now his large excellency the Great Black Cat is here, perhaps your honor wouldn't mind coming down to the kitchen and taking the lid off the big iron pot there. We know it is full of cooked spaghetti, which the steward made before he went away, but the lid is too heavy for us to shift. Your Magnificence will be able to do it easily."

Nero was rather affronted at being given orders by the mice, although they had been very polite about it. He stared at them sharply to make sure they were not poking fun at him.

42

"How do you suggest I get into the kitchen?" he said coldly.

"Why, *ebbene*, down the chimney of course! *Il signore* Nero knows better than anyone in Venice how to do *that*. The fire is out—since many days."

"Yes, that does seem a good idea, Nero," Sandro remarked. "And while you are down in the kitchen you might find other kinds of food that the mice can't reach."

"You won't be *unkind* to any of the mice while you are down there, will you?" Seppi said anxiously. "They are working so hard to save Tomaso."

Nero promised to restrain himself and went off to the chimney stack, which was at the other side of the roof. They heard a heaving and thumping, then nothing more. A considerable time passed.

Sandro began to worry. "I do hope he has not got stuck in the chimney. After all, it is different when his master is there with brushes and ropes."

But presently mice began to emerge from under the door, dragging immense lengths of spaghetti that they had hauled all the way up the stairs from the kitchen. Soon a large, pale pile of it was coiled up in one corner of the attic. From some scuffles and a few curses on the other side of the door, it could be guessed that Nero was helping in this operation but was finding it hard to cooperate with the mice.

After a while he reappeared outside the window, dragging a bunch of very sooty dried sausages, which he pushed through the hole.

"There wasn't much else in the kitchen," he reported. "I daresay the family took most of the food with them

43

when they went to the country. We'll have to arrange for a supply of food from outside."

Since the prisoner was now well supplied for the moment, however, with enough to last him at least for a couple of days, and since everybody was tired out, the mice limped off to their quarters downstairs, and Nero and Sandro prepared to go home. Seppi said that he would spend the night with the patient. Umberto asked, rather diffidently, if someone could take him home, as it was rather a long journey and he was not certain of the way.

"My dear Umberto! Of course I shall see you back to your door," Sandro said graciously.

In consequence of which, an amazed late-night gondolier, poling his craft home along the Grand Canal, found himself beckoned to the quayside by a negligent wave of Sandro's golden tail. "And, would you credit it, there was a *mouse* riding on the cat's back!" he reported later to his wife. "And they *both* got off at the Cappella palace."

"Ernesto, you've had too much chianti again," said his wife, turning over sleepily in bed.

Luckily the drainpipe shared by Seppi and Umberto was only a couple of blocks from the Cappella palace. Sandro carried Umberto to his door as promised, and then went home himself for a well-earned day's sleep. Nero was already curled up on a soot sack in his master's boat, taking a cat nap. But Seppi sat up for the rest of the night, watching the sleeping Tomaso and observing with joy, as dawn approached, that the young man's breathing became slower and easier, his brow was cool, his hands were damp, and the fever had left him. At last, satisfied that the patient would recover, Seppi curled up in a ball, comfortably jammed against Tomaso's chest, and they slept together.

44

The Cat Who Lived in a Drainpipe

They woke together, too, for Tomaso, halfway through the morning, suddenly sat up with a strangled shout, dislodging Seppi, who bounced onto his feet with his fur on end.

"What—what am I doing here?" said the young man confusedly. "I dreamed—I was dreaming I had been alone for days and days. I was starving to death. Was it true? Good heavens," he added, looking around him at all the little heaps of olives and grapes, the rows of carrots and beans, the tastefully arranged little patterns of cherries and chestnuts, of rice and peas, and the pale heap of spaghetti. "Who brought all this? Did Michele?"

"Prrrt," said Seppi.

"Or did you?" said Tomaso, looking at him closely. "How did *you* find your way in here? I know you. You're the little fellow who's always trying to steal a ride on my gondola. Well, I'm happy to have your company now, I can tell you. You are kindly welcome to share my breakfast."

Seppi did not wish to do this, but watched with huge satisfaction as the young man made a good meal of spaghetti and olives, grapes and chestnuts and sausages.

Presently some of the house mice arrived to ask if more supplies were needed yet; they brought with them small lumps of fresh *stracchino* cheese.

"Some friends from outside had heard of the young gentleman's situation, and they sent this in, as they live in a dairy. They wondered if he could use it."

Tomaso watched in utter amazement as the procession of mice rolled pieces of cheese across the floor and Seppi supervised their arrangement on an artichoke leaf.

Then a gull tapped at the window. "Beg pardon, I understand that the young fellow who lives here and plays the violin is in need of a bit of fruit?"

About fifty gulls swooped past, each dropping an orange or a grapefruit onto the roof.

Next a whole flock of pigeons arrived, each bearing some delicacy: a small cake, a shrimp, a sardine.

"We picked these up in the street market," one of them told Seppi. "There's a rumor going around among all the mice of the town that the young musician here is starving. We couldn't have that. Everybody loves his playing."

And a convocation of swans flew by, each bearing an oyster. "With best wishes for the young gentleman's recovery."

And a procession of rats came toiling over the rooftops from a spaghetti factory; Tomaso had enough spaghetti to last him a year, piled up on the roof.

"Seppi," he said in amazement, "you seem to have the whole town organized."

Seppi modestly busied himself in washing his stump of tail; he felt that it was unfair he should receive all the credit.

Three or four days passed in this manner, a week, two weeks. Sandro and Nero returned every evening. But Seppi stayed with Tomaso daylong and nightlong; by day he watched contentedly as Tomaso nibbled at his provisions and slowly grew stronger; by night they both slept curled up together under Tomaso's cloak.

At the end of the first week, Tomaso was sufficiently recovered to begin playing a few tunes on his oboe. And at that, Seppi was flooded by such happiness that he hardly knew how to contain himself. To be able to sit, hour after hour, on the musician's cloak, listening to his marvelously beautiful music! What other cat in the world could possibly have such good fortune?

On the fifteenth day a gull flew over, shouting, "The parents are coming! They are coming along the canal in a gondola!"

Soon there was a confused noise downstairs, of doors opening, bumps and thumps, and loud voices exclaiming in horror.

Then heavy steps running up the stairs. The mice all bolted for cover.

And suddenly the door flew open, after a rattling of key in lock, and in burst Tomaso's father and mother. Their faces were as white as *stracchino* cheese. Plainly they expected to find their son stretched out dead on the floor.

"My son, my son!"

"My darling child!"

"Oh, my dear boy!"

"*Dio mio*, he is safe, he is alive! Heaven be thanked."

They embraced Tomaso over and over. "Oh, my dear child! By what merciful providence are you still with us?" said his father. "Where is Michele? What happened? We had told him to let you out after four days, even if you did not change your mind. And we meant to come back at the end of a week, but your mother fell ill in the country, and we could not leave until yesterday. And we had heard nothing from Michele. What has happened? We found the house empty and all the fires out. *Who* has been feeding you all this time?"

"Quite evidently the blessed saints have been looking after the boy," said his mother, gazing around, with the tears pouring down her face. "Now do you see, Antonio, that he is something special, and that if he wants to marry a girl called Margherita from the orphanage—who, I daresay, is a perfectly nice little thing—he should be allowed to do so?"

"Oh, very well," agreed old Antonio, who, in fact, was so glad to find his dear son still alive that he would have allowed him to marry a mermaid, if one had been at hand. "But was it really the blessed saints who were looking after you, my dear Tomaso?"

"No, Father. It was an ugly little cat with no tail called Seppi."

"A *cat*? Where is he?" cried the mother. "He shall sit on a gold cushion till the end of his days."

But Seppi, scared by all the noise and excitement, had darted in nervous haste out through the window hole, thanking his stars that he had eaten only very politely and sparingly of Tomaso's provisions and was still thin enough to squeeze through. No sign of either him or the mice remained—only a room piled high with olives and chestnuts and cheese.

Tomaso's parents practically carried him downstairs; they wanted to feast him on all the finest delicacies in Venice, but he said he was really full up and could eat nothing more just then. So, instead, they sent a note to the orphanage, asking for the hand of Margherita Rimondi for their son and heir. It was arranged that the young couple should be married two weeks from that day.

A couple of days later, Tomaso's mother said to him, "What is the matter, my son? You look thoughtful. Aren't you quite happy?"

The Cat Who Lived in a Drainpipe

"Well, yes, I am, Mother, happy as the day is long. But I wish I could find that little cat. I wish he hadn't disappeared. It was really he who saved my life."

"Are you sure you didn't dream him in the fever, my son?"

"Oh, I do hope I didn't!" said Tomaso. But then he added, "No, I'm sure I didn't dream him, for I used to find him hiding in my gondola before all this happened."

"Well, then, it should be possible to find him."

In the meantime, where *was* Seppi?

Back in his drainpipe. He had fled to his only refuge, feeling sure that, now the young man's family had returned and all was forgiven, nobody would even spare a thought for a dirty little alley cat with most of his tail missing.

Day after day Seppi stayed crouching in the pipe, damp and melancholy, not even bothering to step outside for a breath of fresh air.

"You really ought to take a bit of exercise, you know," said Umberto disapprovingly from the other end of the pipe. Seppi merely grunted in reply. He was thinking, When Tomaso is married, he might move away from Venice. I may never see him anymore, never hear him play again.

He was very miserable.

And then, one day, he heard a gondola swishing along the canal outside his drainpipe, and he heard Nero's deep bass bellow, "Seppi! Come out of there! Everybody is looking for you!"

Seppi put his head out of the pipe. There was Benno Fosco's boat, full of black sacks, and Nero, sooty, stately, and commanding.

"Come on! Hurry up! Tomaso is getting married to-morrow, and he wants all the friends who helped him when he was a prisoner to join in his wedding procession, and you especially."

"Oh, he won't miss *me*," said Seppi, pulling his head back in again.

"What rubbish! Why, he's had notices put up all over Venice. Wanted to find: Small black-and-white cat with one blue eye, one yellow, and half a tail."

"Really?"

"He wants you to live in his house!"

"Wh-what?"

"And you might just as well," said Nero kindly. "I think it's an excellent scheme. After all, Sandro and I have good homes of our own, but what have you got? A drainpipe! What kind of an establishment is that? Hurry up! Benno can't wait about all day. We've got six customers to take care of."

It was an unforgettable wedding. Gulls and pigeons flew over the bridal gondola. Swans drifted after it. Mice lined the quayside and bridges. And all the cats of Venice were there—perched on sills, on doorsteps, on steps, on skiffs and ferries, on hulls and prows. So many cats together were never seen before or since.

Seppi went to live with Tomaso and Margherita. He slept on a blue velvet cushion. He became brilliantly clean, his white patches like silk and his black like ebony. But he never grew any bigger. He played with all the six children of Tomaso and Margherita as they came along, and his nine lives extended on and on, until they seemed more like ninety-nine. He was happier than any other cat in

Italy, for, alone of all the household, he was allowed into the musician's workroom and could listen to every note that his master—who became a famous composer—ever played.

(But on one night a week, Seppi went out over the roofs and sang in a concert with Sandro and Nero. All the Venetian cats were delighted to have their favorite trio back, and indeed the three became so well known that cats traveled from Milan and even Rome to hear them.)

Several years later Tomaso, now very famous indeed, was invited to visit the duke of Bavaria. And while on this visit, one day in the street, he ran into a man who went chalk-white at the sight of him, fell on his knees, and stammered, "It's n-n-never the young master? Praise be to all the holy saints! I thought you were dead!"

He was Michele, the steward.

He told how he had been knocked unconscious in a street fight and woke to find himself on a ship, where he had been dumped by someone who thought he was a sailor. The ship was already halfway to Africa.

"And when I thought of how you had been left—all alone in the house—oh, I nearly went mad! A week had gone by. I thought you must be dead already. I never dared go back to Venice. I've been in terrible grief all my days, thinking about you and how your father and mother must have felt when they returned. Oh, forgive me, forgive me!"

"Forgive? It was not your fault!" said Tomaso. "Quick! Jump on a horse and hurry back to Venice! You were only doing what you had been ordered."

"I was to let you out after four days!"

"So you would have. You didn't mean to leave me shut

51

up in the attic. But anyway what a good thing you did! For without that, I should never have married. And I would never have found my Seppi!"

NOTE: Tomaso Albinoni, son of a wealthy paper manufacturer, lived in Venice from 1671 to 1750, wrote beautiful music, married Margherita Rimondi, and had six children. There is no record of his having a cat. But he probably did. Venice is full of cats.

The Cat

MARY E. WILKINS FREEMAN

The snow was falling, and the Cat's fur was stiffly pointed with it, but he was imperturbable. He sat crouched, ready for the death spring, as he had sat for hours. It was night —but that made no difference—all times were as one to the Cat when he was in wait for prey. Then, too, he was under no constraint of human will, for he was living alone that winter. Nowhere in the world was any voice calling him; on no hearth was there a waiting dish. He was quite free except for his own desires, which tyrannized over him when unsatisfied as now. The Cat was very hungry—almost famished, in fact. For days the weather had been very bitter, and all the feebler wild things that were his prey by inheritance, the born serfs to his family, had kept, for the most part, in their burrows and nests, and the Cat's long hunt had availed him nothing. But he waited with the inconceivable patience and persistency of his race; besides, he was certain.

The Cat was a creature of absolute convictions, and his faith in his deductions never wavered. The rabbit had gone in there between those low-hung pine boughs. Now her little doorway had before it a shaggy curtain of snow, but in there she was. The Cat had seen her enter, so like a swift gray shadow that even his sharp and practiced eyes had glanced back for the substance following, and then she was gone. So he sat down and waited, and he waited still in the white night, listening angrily to the north wind starting in the upper heights of the mountains with distant screams, then swelling into an awful crescendo of rage, and swooping down with furious white wings of snow like a flock of fierce eagles into the valleys and ravines.

The Cat was on the side of a mountain, on a wooded terrace. Above him a few feet away towered the rock ascent as steep as the wall of a cathedral. The Cat had never climbed it; trees were the ladders to his heights of life. He had often looked with wonder at the rock and miauled bitterly and resentfully as man does in the face of a forbidding Providence. At his left was the sheer precipice. Behind him, with a short stretch of woody growth between, was the frozen perpendicular wall of a mountain stream. Before him was the way to his home. When the rabbit came out she was trapped; her little cloven feet could not scale such unbroken steeps.

So the Cat waited. The place in which he was looked

The Cat

like a maelstrom of the wood. The tangle of trees and bushes clinging to the mountainside with a stern clutch of roots, the prostrate trunks and branches, the vines embracing everything with strong knots and coils of growth, had a curious effect, as of things that had whirled for ages in a current of raging water; only it was not water, but wind, that had disposed everything in circling lines of yielding to its fiercest points of onset. And now over all this whirl of wood and rock and dead trunks and branches and vines descended the snow. It blew down like smoke over the rock crest above; it stood in a gyrating column like some death wraith of nature, on the level; then it broke over the edge of the precipice, and the Cat cowered before the fierce backward set of it. It was as if ice needles pricked his skin through his beautiful, thick fur, but he never faltered and never once cried. He had nothing to gain from crying, and everything to lose; the rabbit would hear him cry and know he was waiting.

It grew darker and darker, with a strange white smother, instead of the natural blackness of night. It was a night of storm and death superadded to the night of nature. The mountains were all hidden, wrapped about, overawed, and tumultuously overborne by it, but in the midst of it waited, quite unconquered, this little, unswerving, living patience and power under a little coat of gray fur.

A fiercer blast swept over the rock, spun on one mighty foot of whirlwind athwart the level, then was over the precipice.

At that moment the Cat saw two eyes luminous with terror, frantic with the impulse of flight. He saw a little, quivering, dilating nose, he saw two pointing ears, and he kept still, with every one of his fine nerves and muscles strained like wires. Then the rabbit was out—there was one long line of incarnate flight and terror—and the Cat had her.

Finally the Cat went home, trailing his prey through the snow.

The Cat lived in the house that his master had built, as rudely as a child's blockhouse, but staunchly enough. The snow was heavy on the low slant of its roof, but it would not settle under it. The two windows and the door were made fast, but the Cat knew a way in. Up a pine tree behind the house he scuttled, though it was hard work with his heavy rabbit, and was in his little window under the eaves, then down through the trap to the room below, and on his master's bed with a spring and a great cry of triumph, rabbit and all. But his master was not there; he had been gone since early fall and it was now February. He would not return until spring, for he was an old man, and the cruel cold of the mountains clutched at his vitals like a panther, and he had gone to the village to winter. The Cat had known for a long time that his master was gone, but his reasoning was always sequential and circuitous; always for him what had been would be, and the more easily for his marvelous waiting powers so he always came home expecting to find his master.

When he saw that he was still gone, he dragged the rabbit off the rude couch that was the bed to the floor, put one little paw on the carcass to keep it steady, and began gnawing with head to one side to bring his strongest teeth to bear.

It was darker in the house than it had been in the wood, and the cold was as deadly, though not so fierce. If the Cat had not received his fur coat unquestioningly of Provi-

56

dence, he would have been thankful that he had it. It was a mottled gray, white on the face and breast, and thick as fur could grow.

The wind drove the snow on the windows with such force that it rattled like sleet, and the house trembled a little. All at once the Cat heard a noise and stopped gnawing his rabbit and listened, his shining green eyes fixed upon a window. Then he heard a hoarse shout, a halloo of despair and entreaty. But he knew it was not his master come home, and he waited, one paw still on the rabbit. The halloo came again, and then the Cat answered. He said all that was essential quite plainly to his own comprehension. There was in his cry of response inquiry, information, warning, terror, and finally the offer of comradeship, but the man outside did not hear him because of the howling of the storm.

Then there was a great battering pound at the door, then another, and another. The Cat dragged his rabbit under the bed. The blows came thicker and faster. It was a weak arm that gave them, but it was nerved by desperation. Finally the lock yielded, and the stranger came in. Then the Cat, peering from under the bed, blinked with a sudden light, and his green eyes narrowed. The stranger struck a match and looked about. The Cat saw a face wild and blue with hunger and cold, and a man who looked poorer and older than his poor old master, who was an outcast among men for his poverty and lowly mystery of antecedents, and he heard a muttered, unintelligible voicing of distress from the harsh piteous mouth. There was in it both profanity and prayer, but the Cat knew nothing of that.

The stranger braced the door that he had forced, got

some wood from the stock in the corner, and kindled a fire in the old stove as quickly as his half-frozen hands would allow. He shook so pitiably as he worked that the Cat under the bed felt the tremor of it. Then the man, who was small and feeble and marked with the scars of suffering that he had pulled down upon his own head, sat down in one of the old chairs and crouched over the fire as if it were the one love and desire of his soul, holding out his yellow hands like yellow claws, and he groaned. The Cat came out from under the bed and leaped up on his lap with the rabbit. The man gave a great shout and start of terror, and sprang. The Cat slid clawing to the floor, the rabbit fell inertly, and the man leaned, gasping with fright, and ghastly, against the wall. The Cat grabbed the rabbit by the slack of its neck and dragged it to the man's feet. Then he raised his shrill, insistent cry and arched his back high, his tail a splendid waving plume. He rubbed against the man's feet, which were bursting out of their torn shoes.

The man pushed the Cat away, gently enough, and began searching about the little cabin. He even painfully climbed the ladder to the loft, lit a match, and peered up in the darkness with straining eyes. He feared lest there might be a man, since there was a cat. His experience with men had not been pleasant, and neither had the experience of men been pleasant with him. He was an old wandering Ishmael among his kind; he had stumbled upon the house of a brother, and the brother was not at home, and he was glad.

He returned to the Cat, stooped stiffly, and stroked his back, which the animal arched like the spring of a bow.

58

The Cat

Then he took up the rabbit and looked at it eagerly by the firelight. His jaws worked. He could almost have devoured it raw. He fumbled—the Cat close at his heels—around some rude shelves and a table, and found, with a grunt of self-gratulation, a lamp with oil in it. That he lighted; then he found a frying pan and a knife, skinned the rabbit, and prepared it for cooking, the Cat always at his feet.

When the odor of the cooking flesh filled the cabin, both the man and the Cat looked wolfish. The man turned the rabbit with one hand and stooped to pat the Cat with the other. The Cat thought him a fine man. He loved him with all his heart, though he had known him such a short time, and though the man had a face both pitiful and sharply set at variance with the best of things.

It was a face with the grimy grizzle of age upon it, with fever hollows in the cheeks, and the memories of wrong in the dim eyes, but the Cat accepted the man unquestioningly and loved him. When the rabbit was half cooked, neither the man nor the Cat would wait any longer. The man took it from the fire, divided it exactly in halves, gave the Cat one, and took the other himself. Then they ate.

At last the man blew out the light, called the Cat to him, got on the bed, drew up the ragged coverings, and fell asleep with the Cat in his bosom.

The man was the Cat's guest all the rest of the winter, and winter is long in the mountains. The rightful owner of the little hut did not return until May. All that time the Cat toiled hard, and he grew rather thin himself, for he shared everything except mice with his guest. Sometimes game was wary, and the fruit of patience of days was very little for two. The man was ill and weak, however, and unable to eat much, which was fortunate, since he could not hunt for himself. All day long he lay on the bed or else sat crouched over the fire. It was a good thing that firewood was ready at hand for the picking up, not a stone's throw from the door, for that he had to attend to himself.

The Cat foraged tirelessly. Sometimes he was gone for days together, and at first the man used to be terrified, thinking he would never return. Then he would hear the familiar cry at the door, stumble to his feet, and let him in. Afterward the two would dine together, sharing equally; the Cat would rest and purr and finally sleep in the man's arms.

Toward spring the game grew plentiful; more wild little quarry were tempted out of their homes, in search of love as well as food. One day the Cat had luck—a rabbit, a partridge, and a mouse. He could not carry them all at once, but finally he had them together at the house door. Then he cried, but no one answered. All the mountain streams were loosened, and the air was full of the gurgle of many waters, occasionally pierced by a bird whistle. The trees rustled with a new sound to the spring wind; there was a flush of rose and gold-green on the breasting surface of a distant mountain seen through an opening in the wood. The tips of the bushes were swollen and glistening red, and now and then there was a flower, but the Cat had nothing to do with flowers. He stood beside his booty at the house door and cried and cried with his insistent triumph and complaint and pleading, but no one came to let him in. Then the Cat left his little treasures at the door, went around to the back of the house to the pine tree, was

60

up the trunk with a wild scramble, in through his little window, and down through the trap to the room, and the man was gone.

The Cat cried again, that cry of the animal for human companionship that is one of the sad notes of the world; he looked in all the corners; he sprang to the chair at the window and looked out. But no one came. The man was gone, and he never came again.

The Cat ate his mouse out on the turf beside the house; the rabbit and the partridge he carried painfully into the house. But the man did not come to share them. Finally, in the course of a day or two, he ate them up himself; then he slept a long time on the bed, and when he waked the man was not there.

Then the Cat went forth to his hunting grounds again and came home at night with a plump bird, reasoning with his tireless persistency in expectancy that the man would be there, and there was a light in the window. When he cried, his old master opened the door and let him in.

His master had strong comradeship with the Cat, but not affection. He never patted him like that gentler outcast, but he had a pride in him and an anxiety for his welfare, though he had left him alone all winter without scruple. He feared lest some misfortune might have come to the Cat, though he was so large of his kind and a mighty hunter. Therefore, when he saw him at the door in all the glory of his glossy winter coat, his white breast and face shining like snow in the sun, his own face lit up with welcome, and the Cat embraced his feet with his sinuous body vibrant with rejoicing purrs.

The Cat had his bird to himself, for his master had his

own supper already cooking on the stove. After supper the
Cat's master took his pipe and sought a small store of tobacco that he had left in his hut over winter. He had
thought often of it; that and the Cat seemed something to
come home to in the spring. But the tobacco was gone,
not a dust left. The man swore a little in a grim monotone,
which made the profanity lose its customary effect. He had
been, and was, a hard drinker; he had knocked about the
world until the marks of its sharp corners were on his very
soul, which was thereby calloused until his very sensibility
to loss was dulled. He was a very old man.

He searched for the tobacco with a sort of dull com-
bativeness of persistency; then he stared with stupid wonder around the room. Suddenly many features struck him
as being changed. Another stove lid was broken; an old
piece of carpet was tacked up over a window to keep out
the cold; his firewood was gone. He looked and there was
no oil left in his can. He looked at the coverings on his
bed; he took them up, and again he made that strange
remonstrant noise in his throat. Then he looked again for
his tobacco.

Finally he gave it up. He sat down beside the fire, for
May in the mountains is cold; he held his empty pipe in
his mouth, his rough forehead knitted, and he and the Cat
looked at each other across that impassable barrier of silence
that has been set between man and beast from the creation
of the world.

The Ginger King

A. E. W. MASON

Monsieur Hanaud was smoking one of Mr. Ricardo's special Havanas in the dining room of Mr. Ricardo's fine house in Grosvenor Square. The trial that had fetched him over from Paris had ended that morning. He had eaten a very good lunch with his friend, he had taken the napkin down from his collar, he was at his ease, and as he smoked, alas! he preached.

"Chance, my friend, is the detective's best confederate. A little unimportant word you use and it startles—a strange twist of character is provoked to reveal itself—an odd incident breaks in on the routine of your investigation. And the mind pounces. 'Ping,' you say, if you play table tennis. 'Pong,' you say, if you play the Mah-Jongg. And there you are! In at the brush."

"I beg your pardon."

For the moment Mr. Ricardo was baffled.

"I said, 'You are in at the brush,'" Hanaud repeated amiably.

Mr. Ricardo smiled with indulgence. He too had eaten his share of an admirable saddle of lamb and drunk his half of a bottle of exquisite Haut Brion.

"You mean, of course, that you are in at the death," he said.

"No, no," Hanaud protested, starting forward. "I do not speak of executions. Detectives are never present at executions, and, for me, I find them disgusting. I say, you are in at the brush. It is an idiom from your hunting field. It means that when all the mess is swept up you are *there*, the Man who found the Lady under the thimble."

Mr. Ricardo was in no mood to pursue his large friend through the winding mazes of his metaphors. "I am beginning to understand you," he answered with resignation.

"Yes." Hanaud nodded his head complacently. "I speak the precision. It is known."

With a gentle knock, Mr. Ricardo's incomparable butler Thomson entered the room. "A Mr. Middleton has called," he said, offering to Ricardo a visiting card upon a salver.

Ricardo waved the salver away. "I do not see visitors immediately after luncheon. It is an unforgivable time to call. Send him away!"

The butler, however, persisted. "I took the liberty of

pointing out that the hour was unseasonable," he said, "but Mr. Middleton was in hopes that Monsieur Hanaud was staying with you. He seemed very anxious."

Ricardo took up the card reluctantly. He read aloud, "'Mr. John Middleton, Secretary of the Unicorn Fire Insurance Company.' I am myself insured with that firm." He turned toward his guest. "No doubt he has some reason to excuse him. But it is as you wish."

Monsieur Hanaud's strange ambition that afternoon was to climb the Monument and to see the Crown Jewels at the Tower, but his good nature won the day, and, since he was to find more than one illustration of the text upon which he had been preaching, he never regretted it. "I am on view," he said simply.

"We will see Mr. Middleton in the library," said Mr. Ricardo, and into that spacious dormitory of deep armchairs and noble books Mr. Middleton was introduced.

Hanaud was delighted with the look of him. Mr. Middleton was a collector's piece of Victorian England. Middle-aged, with dangling whiskers like lappets at the sides of an otherwise clean-shaven face, very careful and a trifle old-maidish in his speech, he had a tittering laugh and wore the long black frock coat and the striped trousers that once made London what it was. He was wreathed in apologies for his intrusion.

"My good friend Superintendent Holloway, of Marlborough Street, whose little property is insured with us, thought that I might find you at Mr. Ricardo's house. I am very fortunate."

"I must return to Paris tomorrow," Hanaud replied. "For this afternoon I am at your service. You will smoke?"

65

From his pocket Hanaud tendered a bright blue packet of black stringy cigarettes, and Mr. Middleton recoiled as if he suddenly saw a cobra on the carpet ready to strike.

"Oh, no, no!" he cried in dismay. "A small mild cigar when the day's work is done. You will forgive me? I have a little story to tell."

"Proceed!" said Hanaud graciously.

"It is a Mr. Enoch Swallow," Mr. Middleton began. "I beg you not to be misled by his name. He is a Syrian gentleman by birth and an English gentleman by naturalization. But again I beg you not to be misled. There is nothing of the cunning of the Orient about him. He is a big, plain, simple creature, a peasant, one might say as honest as the day. And it may be so. I make no accusation."

"He has a business, this honest man?" Hanaud asked.

"He is a furrier."

"You begin to interest me," said Hanaud.

"A year ago Enoch Swallow fitted up for his business a house in Berwick Street, toward the Oxford Street end of that long and narrow thoroughfare. The ground floor became his showrooms, he and his wife with a cook-general to wait on them occupied the first floor, and the two stories above were elaborately arranged for his valuable stock. Then he came to us for an insurance policy."

"Aha!" said Monsieur Hanaud.

"We hesitated," continued Mr. Middleton, stroking one of his side-whiskers. "Everything was as it should be—the lease of the house, compliance with the regulations of the county council, the value of the stock—mink, silver fox, sables—all correct, and yet we hesitated."

"Why?" asked Hanaud.

"Mind, I make no suggestion." Mr. Middleton was very

insistent upon his complete detachment. "It was held to be an accident. The Société Universelle paid the insurance money. But Mr. Enoch Swallow did have a fire in a similar establishment on the Boulevard Haussmann in Paris three years before."

"Enoch Swallow? The Boulevard Haussmann?" Hanaud dived deep among his memories but came to the surface with empty hands. "No, I do not remember. There was no case."

"Oh, dear me, no," Mr. Middleton insisted. "Oh, none at all. Fires happen, else why does one insure? So in the end—it is our business and competition is severe and nothing could have been more straightforward than the conduct of our client—we insured him."

"For a large sum?"

"For twenty-five thousand pounds."

Hanaud whistled. He multiplied the amount into francs. It became milliards.

"For a Syrian gentleman, even if he is now an English gentleman, it is a killing."

"And then last night it all happens again," cried Mr. Middleton, giving his whisker a twist and a slap. "Would you believe it?"

"I certainly would," replied Hanaud, "and without bringing the least pressure upon my credulity."

Mr. Middleton raised a warning hand. "But remember, please, there is no accusation. No. All is above board. No smell of petrol in the ruins. No little machine with an alarm clock. Nothing."

"And yet," said Hanaud with a smile, "you have your little thoughts."

The secretary tittered. "Monsieur Hanaud," he said

coyly, "I have in my day been something of a dasher. I went once to the Moulin Rouge. I tried once to smoke a stringy black cigarette from a blue packet. But the strings got between my teeth and caused me extreme discomfort. Well, today I have Mr. Enoch Swallow between my teeth."

Mr. Ricardo, who all this time had been sitting silent, thought it a happy moment to make a little jest that if the secretary swallowed Mr. Swallow he would suffer even more discomfort. But though Middleton tittered dutifully, Hanaud looked a thousand reproaches and Mr. Ricardo subsided.

"I want to hear of last night," said Hanaud.

It was the cook-general's night out. She had permission, moreover, to stay the night with friends at Balham. She had asked for that permission herself. No hint had been given to her that her absence would be welcome. Her friends had invited her, and she had sought for this leave on her own initiative.

"Well, then," continued Mr. Middleton, "at six o'clock she laid a cold supper for the Swallows in the dining room and took an omnibus to Balham. The employees had already gone. The showrooms were closed, and only Enoch Swallow and his wife were left in the house. At seven those two ate their supper, and after locking the front door behind them went to a cinema house in Oxford Street where a French film was being shown. *Toto et Fils* was the name of the film."

They arrived at the cinema house a few minutes past eight. There was no doubt whatever about that. For they met the manager of the house, with whom they were acquainted, in the lobby and talked with him while they waited for the earlier performance to end and its audience to disperse. They had seats in the Grand Circle, and there the manager found them just before eleven o'clock, when he brought them the news that their premises were on fire.

"Yes, the incontestable alibi," said Hanaud. "I was waiting for him."

"They hurried home," Middleton resumed, but Hanaud would not allow the word.

"Home? Have such people a home? A place full of little valueless treasures that you would ache to lose? The history of your small triumphs, your great griefs, your happy hours? No, no, we keep to facts. They had a store and a shop and a lodging, and they come back and it is all in flames. Good! We continue. When was this fire first noticed?"

"About half past nine a passerby saw the smoke curling out from the door. He crossed the street, and he saw a flame shoot up and spread behind a window—he thinks on the first floor. But he will not swear that it wasn't on the second. It took him a few minutes to find one of the red pillars where you give the alarm by breaking the glass. The summer has been dry; all those painted pitch-pine shelves in the upper stories were like tinder. By the time the fire brigade arrived the house was a bonfire. By the time the Swallows were discovered in the cinema and ran back to Berwick Street the floors were crashing down. When the cook-general returned at six-thirty this morning, it was a ruin of debris and tottering walls."

"And the Swallows?" Hanaud asked.

"They had lost everything. They had nothing but the

clothes they were wearing. They were taken in for the night at a little hotel in Percy Street."

"The poor people!" said Hanaud with a voice of commiseration and a face like a mask. "And how do they explain the fire?"

"They do not," said Middleton. "The good wife she weeps, the man is distressed and puzzled. He was most careful, he says, and, since the fire did not start until some time after he and his wife had left the house, he thinks some burglar is to blame. Ah, yes!" Mr. Middleton pushed himself forward on his chair. "There is a little something. He suggests—it is not very nice—that the burglar may have been a friend of the cook-general. He has no evidence. No. He used to think her a simple, honest, stupid woman and not a good cook, but now he is not sure. No, it is not a nice suggestion."

"But we must remember that he was a Syrian gentleman before he became an English one, must we not?" said Hanaud. "Yes, such suggestions were certainly to be expected. You have seen him?"

"Of course," cried Mr. Middleton, and he edged so much more forward in his chair that it seemed he must topple off. "And I should esteem it a favor if you, Monsieur Hanaud, and your friend Mr. Ricardo"—he gathered the derelict Ricardo gracefully into the council—"would see him too."

Hanaud raised his hands in protest. "It would be an irregularity of the most extreme kind. I have no place in this affair. I am the smelly outsider." And by lighting one of his acrid cigarettes he substantiated his position.

Mr. Middleton waved the epithet and the argument away. He would never think of compromising Monsieur

Hanaud. He meant "see" and not examine, and here his friend Superintendent Holloway had come to his help. The superintendent had also wished to see Mr. Enoch Swallow. He had no charge to bring against Enoch. To Superintendent Holloway, as superintendent, Enoch Swallow was the victim of misfortune, insured of course, but still a victim. None the less the superintendent wanted to have a look at him. He had accordingly asked him to call at the Marlborough Street police station at five o'clock.

"You see, the superintendent has a kindly, pleasant reason for his invitation. Mr. Swallow will be grateful and the superintendent will see him. Also you, Monsieur Hanaud, from the privacy of the superintendent's office can see him too and perhaps—who knows—a memory may be jogged?"

Mr. Middleton stroked a whisker and smiled ingratiatingly.

"After all, twenty-five thousand pounds! It is a sum."

"It is the whole multiplication table," Hanaud agreed.

He hesitated for a moment. There was the Monument; there were the Crown Jewels. On the other hand, he liked Mr. Middleton's polite, engaging ways, he liked his whiskers and his frock coat. Also he, too, would like to see the Syrian gentleman. For. . . .

"He is either a very honest unlucky man, or he had a formula for fireworks." Hanaud looked at the clock. It was four.

"We have an hour. I make you a proposal. We will go to Berwick Street and see these ruins, though that beautiful frock coat will suffer."

Mr. Middleton beamed. "It would be worth many frock coats to see Monsieur Hanaud at work," he exclaimed, and

71

thereupon Mr. Ricardo made rather tartly—for undoubtedly he had been neglected—his one effective contribution to this story.

"But the frock coat won't suffer, Mr. Middleton. Ask Hanaud! It will be in at the brush!"

To north and south of the house, Berwick Street had been roped off against the danger of those tottering walls. The salvage company had been at work since the early morning clearing the space within, but there were still beams insecurely poised overhead, and a litter of broken furniture and burned furrier's stock encumbered the ground. Middleton's pass gave them admittance into the shell of the building. Hanaud looked around with the pleased admiration of a connoisseur for an artist's masterpiece.

"Aha!" he said brightly. "I fear that Misters the Unicorn pay twenty-five thousand pounds. It is of an admirable completeness, this fire. We say either 'What a misfortune!' or 'What a formula!'"

He advanced, very wary of the joists and beams balanced above his head, but shirking none of them. "You will not follow me, please," he said to Ricardo and Middleton. "It is not for your safety. But, as my friend Ricardo knows, too many cooks and I'm down the drain."

He went forward and about, mapping out from the fragments of inner walls the lie of the rooms. Once he stopped and came back to the two visitors.

"There was electric light, of course," he said rather than asked. "I can see here and there plugs and pipes."

"There was nothing but electric light and power," Middleton replied firmly. "The cooking was done on an electric stove, and the wires were all carried in steel tubes.

Since the store and the stock were inflammable, we took particular care that these details were carried out."

Hanaud returned to his pacing. At one place a heavy iron bath had crashed through the first-floor ceiling to the ground, its white paint burned off and its pipes twisted by the heat. At this bath he stopped again, raised his head into the air and sniffed, then bent down toward the ground and sniffed again. He stood up with a look of perplexity upon his face, a man trying to remember and completely baffled.

He moved away from this center in various directions as though he was walking outward along the spokes of a wheel, but he always came back to it. Finally he stooped and began to examine some broken lumps of glass that lay about and in the bath. It seemed to the watchers that he picked one of these pieces up, turned it over in his hands, held it beneath his nose and finally put it away in one of his pockets. He returned to his companions.

"We must be at Marlborough Street at five," he said. "Let us go!"

Mr. Ricardo at the rope barrier signaled to a taxi driver. They climbed into it and sat in a row, both Middleton and Ricardo watching Hanaud expectantly, Hanaud sitting between them very upright with no more expression upon his face than has the image of an Egyptian king.

At last he spoke. "I tell you something."

A sigh of relief from Mr. Middleton. Mr. Ricardo smiled and looked proud. His friend was certainly the Man who found the Lady under the thimble.

"Yes, I tell you. The Syrian gentleman has become an English gentleman. He owns a bath."

Mr. Middleton groaned. Ricardo shrugged his shoulders.

It was a deplorable fact that Hanaud never knew when not to be funny.

"But you smelled something," said Mr. Middleton reproachfully.

"You definitely sniffed," said Ricardo.

"Twice," Mr. Middleton insisted.

"Three times," replied Hanaud.

"Ah!" cried Ricardo. "I know. It was petrol."

"Yes!" exclaimed Mr. Middleton excitedly. "Petrol stored secretly in the bath."

Hanaud shook his head. "Not 'arf," he said. "No, but perhaps I sniff"—and he laid a hand upon an arm of each of his companions—"a formula. But here we are, are we not? I see a policeman at a door."

They had indeed reached Marlborough Street police station. A constable raised the flap of a counter, and they passed into a large room. An inner door opened, and Superintendent Holloway appeared on the threshold, a large man with his hair speckled with gray and a genial, intelligent face.

"Monsieur Hanaud!" he said, coming forward with an outstretched hand. "This is a pleasant moment for me."

"And the same to you," said Hanaud in his best English.

"You had better perhaps come into my room," the superintendent continued. "Mr. Swallow has not yet arrived."

He led his visitors into a comfortable office and, shutting the door, invited them all to be seated. A large—everything about the Marlborough Street police station seemed to Hanaud to be large—a large beautiful ginger cat with amber-colored lambent eyes lay with his paws doubled up under his chest on a fourth chair and surveyed the party with a godlike indifference.

74

The Ginger King

"You will understand, Monsieur Hanaud," said the superintendent, "that I have nothing against Mr. Swallow at all. But I thought that I would like to see him, and I had an excellent excuse for asking him to call. I like to see people."

"I too," Hanaud answered politely. "I am of the sociables."

"You will have the advantage over me of seeing without being seen," said the superintendent, and he broke off with an exclamation.

The ginger cat had risen from the chair and jumped down onto the floor. There it stretched out one hind leg and then the other, deliberately, as though it had the whole day for that and nothing else. Next it stepped daintily across the floor to Hanaud, licked like a dog the hand that he dropped to stroke it, and then sprang onto his knee and settled down. Settled down, however, is not the expression. It kept its head in the air and looked about in a curious excitement while its brown eyes shone like jewels.

"Well, upon my word," said the superintendent. "That's the first time that cat has recognized the existence of anyone in the station. But there it is. All cats are snobs."

It was a pretty compliment, and doubtless Monsieur Hanaud would have found a fitting reply had not the constable in the outer office raised his voice.

"If you'll come through and take a seat, sir, I'll tell the superintendent," he was heard to say, and Holloway rose to his feet.

"I'll leave the door ajar," he said in a low voice, and he went into the outer office.

Through the slit left open, Hanaud and Ricardo saw

Enoch Swallow rise from his chair. He was a tall, broad man, almost as tall and broad as the superintendent himself, with black short hair and a flat, open, peasant face.

"You wished to see me?" he asked. He had a harsh metallic voice, but the question itself was ordinary and civil. The man was neither frightened nor arrogant nor indeed curious.

"Yes," replied the superintendent. "I must apologize for asking you to call at a time that must be very inconvenient to you. But we have something of yours."

"Something of mine?" asked Mr. Swallow, perhaps a little more slowly than was quite natural.

"Yes," said the superintendent briskly, "and I thought that you would probably like it returned to you at once."

"Of course. I thank you very much. I thought we had lost everything. What is it?" asked Mr. Swallow.

"A cat," the superintendent answered, and Mr. Swallow stood with his mouth open and the color ebbing from his cheeks. The change in him was astonishing. A moment before he had been at his ease, confident, a trifle curious; now he was a man struck out of his wits. He watched the superintendent with dazed eyes, he swallowed, and his face was the color of dirty parchment.

"Yes, a big ginger cat," Holloway continued easily, "with the disdain of an emperor. But the poor beast wasn't disdainful last night, I can tell you. As soon as the door was broken in—you had a pretty good door, Mr. Swallow, and a pretty strong lock—no burglars for you, Mr. Swallow, eh?" The superintendent laughed genially. "Well, as soon as it was broken in, the cat scampered out and ran up one of my officer's legs under his cape and clung there, whim-

76

pering and shaking and terrified out of his senses. And I don't wonder. It had a near shave of a cruel death."

"And you have it here, Superintendent?"

"Yes. I brought it here, gave it some milk, and it has owned my room ever since."

Enoch Swallow sat down again in his chair, and rather suddenly, for his knees were shaking. He gave one rather furtive look around the room and the ceiling. Then he said, "I am grateful."

But he became aware with the mere speaking of the words that his exhibition of emotion required an ampler apology. "I explain to you," he said, spreading out his hands. "For me cats are not so important. But my poor wife—she loves them. All last night, all today, she has made great trouble for me over the loss of our cat. In her mind she saw it burned, its fur first sparks then flames. Horrible!" Enoch Swallow shut his eyes. "Now that it is found unhurt she will be happy. My store, my stock all gone, pouf! Of no consequence. But the Ginger King back again, all is well." With a broad smile Enoch Swallow called the whole station to join him in a humorous appreciation of the eccentricities of women.

"Right!" the superintendent exclaimed. "I'll fetch the Ginger King for you."

At once all Enoch Swallow's muscles tightened and up went his hand in the air. "Wait, please!" he cried. "There is a shop in Regent Street where they sell everything. I will run there and buy a basket with a lid for the Ginger King. Then you shall strap him in and I will take him to my wife, and tonight there will be no unpleasantness. One little moment!"

77

Mr. Enoch Swallow backed out of the entrance and was gone. Superintendent Holloway returned to his office with all the geniality gone from his face. He was frowning heavily.

"Did you ever see that man before, Monsieur Hanaud?" he asked.

"Never," said Hanaud decisively.

The superintendent shook his head. "Funny! That's what I call him. Yes, funny."

Mr. Ricardo laughed in a superior way. There was no problem for him. " 'Some that are mad if they behold a cat,' " he quoted. "Really, really our William knew everything."

Monsieur Hanaud caught him up quickly. "Yes, this Enoch Swallow, he hates a cat. He has the cat complex. He grows green at the thought that he must carry a cat in a basket, yes. Yet he has a cat in the house, he submits to a cat that he cannot endure without being sick, because his wife loves it! Do you think it likely? Again I say 'not 'arf.' "

A rattle and creak of wickerwork against the raised flap of the counter in the outer office announced Enoch Swallow's return.

The superintendent picked up the Ginger King and walked with it into the outer office. Mr. Ricardo, glancing through the open doorway, saw Mr. Swallow's dark face turn actually green. The sergeant at the desk, indeed, thought that he was going to faint and started forward. Enoch Swallow caught hold of himself. He held out the basket to the superintendent.

"If you will put him into it and strap the lid down, it will be all right. I make myself ridiculous," he said with

The Ginger King

a feeble attempt at a smile. "A big strong fellow whose stomach turns over at the sight of a cat? But it is so."

The Ginger King resented the indignity of being imprisoned in a basket; it struggled and spat and bit as if it were the most communistic of cats, but the superintendent and the sergeant between them got it strapped down at last.

"I'll tell you what I'll do, sir," said Holloway. "I'll send the little brute by one of my men around to your hotel—Percy Street, wasn't it?—and then you won't be bothered with it at all."

But Enoch wouldn't hear of putting the station to so much trouble. "Oh, no, no! You are kindness itself, Superintendent. But once he is in the basket I shall not mind him. I shall take him home at once, and my wife will keep him away from me. It is all right. See, I will carry him."

Enoch Swallow certainly did carry him, but very gingerly, and with the basket held well away from his side.

"It would be no trouble to send him along," the superintendent urged, but again the Syrian refused, and with the same vehemence that he had shown before. The police had work to do. It would humiliate him to interfere with it for so small a reason.

"I have after all not very far to go," he said. Then, with still more effusive protestations of his gratitude, he backed out of the police station.

The superintendent returned to his office. "He wouldn't let me send it home for him," he said. He was a very mystified man. "Funny! That's what I call it. Yes, funny." He looked up and broke off suddenly. "Hallo! Where's Monsieur Hanaud gone to?"

Both Middleton and Ricardo had been watching the

scene in the outer office through the crack in the door. Neither of them had seen or heard Hanaud go. There was a second door that opened on the passage to the street, and by that second door Hanaud had slipped away.

"I am sorry," said the superintendent, a little stiffly. "I should have liked to say good-bye to him."

The superintendent was hurt, and Mr. Ricardo hastened to reassure him. "It wasn't discourtesy," he said staunchly. "Hanaud has manners. There is some reason."

Middleton and Ricardo returned to the latter's house in Grosvenor Square, and there, a little more than an hour afterward, Hanaud rejoined them. To their amazement he was carrying Enoch Swallow's basket, and from the basket he took out a contented, purring, gracious Ginger King.

"A little milk, perhaps?" Hanaud suggested. And, having lapped up the milk, the Ginger King mounted a chair, turned in his paws under his chest, and once more surveyed the world with indifferent eyes.

Hanaud explained his sudden departure. "I could not understand why this man who could not abide a cat refused to let the superintendent send it home for him. No, however much he shivered and puked, he would carry it home himself. I had a little thought in my mind that he didn't mean to carry it home at all. So I slipped out into the street and waited for him and followed him. He had never seen me. It was as easy as the alphabet. He walked in a great hurry down to the Charing Cross Road and past the Trafalgar Square and along the Avenue of Northumberland. At the bottom of the Avenue of Northumberland there is—what? Yes, you have guessed him.

The Ginger King

The River Thames. 'Aha,' I say to myself, 'my friend Enoch, you are going to drown the Ginger King. But I, Hanaud, will not allow it. For if you are so anxious to drown him, the Ginger King has something to tell us.'

"So I close up upon his heels. He crossed the road, he leaned over the parapet, swinging the basket carelessly in his hand as though he was thinking of some important matter and not of the Ginger King at all. He looked on this side and that, and then I slip my hand under the basket from behind, and I say in his ear, 'Sir, you will drop that basket, if you don't look out.'

"Enoch, he gave a great jump, and he drop the basket, this time by accident. But my hand is under it. Then I take it by the handle, I make a bow, I hand it to him. I say 'Dr. Livingstone, I presume?' and lifting my hat, I walk away. But not so far. I see him black in the face with rage. But he dare not try the river again. He thinks for a little. Then he crosses the road and dashes through the Underground station. I follow as before. But now he has seen me. He knows my dial," and at Middleton's surprised expression he added, "—my face. It is a little English idiom I use. So I keep farther back, but I do not lose him. He runs up that steep street. Halfway up, he turns to the right."

"John Street," said Mr. Ricardo.

"Halfway up John Street there is a turning to the left under a building. It is a tunnel and dark. Enoch races into the tunnel. I follow, and just as I come to the mouth of it the Ginger King comes flashing out like a strip of yellow lightning. You see, he could not drown him, so in the dark tunnel he turns him loose, with a kick no doubt to make him go. The Ginger King is no longer, if he ever was, the pet of the sad Mrs. Swallow. He is just a stray cat. Dogs will set on him; no one will find him; all the time he must run and very soon he will die.

"But this time he does not need to run. He sees or smells a friend, Hanaud of the Sûreté, that joke, that comic—eh, my friend?" He dug a fist into Ricardo's ribs that made that fastidious gentleman bend like a sapling in a wind. "Ah, you do not like the familiarities. But the Ginger King to the contrary. He stops, he mews, he arches his back and rubs his body against Hanaud's leg. So I pick him up, and I go on into the tunnel. It winds, and at the point where it bends I find the basket with the lid. It is logical. Enoch has dismissed the Ginger King. Therefore, he wants nothing to remind him of the Ginger King. He drops the basket. I insert the Ginger King once more. He has confidence; he does not struggle. I strap down the lid. I come out of the tunnel. I am in the Strand. I look right and left and everywhere. There is no Enoch. I call a taximan."

"And you are here," said Ricardo, who thought the story had been more than sufficiently prolonged. But Hanaud shook his head.

"No, I am not here yet. There are matters of importance in between."

"Very well," said Ricardo languidly. "Proceed."

And Hanaud proceeded. "I put the basket on the seat, and I say to the taximan, 'I want'—guess what?—but you will not guess. 'I want the top-dog chemist.' The taximan wraps himself round and round with clothes, and we arrive at the top-dog chemist. There I get just the information that I need, and now, my friend Ricardo, here I am with the

82

The Ginger King

Ginger King, who sits with a Chinese face and will tell us nothing of what he knows."

But he was unjust. For later on that evening, in his own good time, the Ginger King told them plenty.

They were sitting at dinner at a small mahogany table bright with silver and fine glass: Mr. Ricardo between Hanaud and Middleton, and opposite to Ricardo, with his head just showing above the mahogany, the Ginger King. Suddenly one of those little chancy things upon which Hanaud had preached his sermon happened. The electric light went out.

They sat in the darkness, their voices silenced. Outside the windows the traffic rumbled by, suddenly important. An unreasonable suspense stole into the three men, and they sat very still and aware that each was breathing as lightly as he could. Perhaps for three minutes this odd tension lasted, and then the invaluable Thomson came into the room carrying a lighted lamp. It was an old-fashioned oil affair with a round of baize cloth under the base, a funnel, and an opaque globe in the heart of which glowed a red flame.

"A fuse has blown, sir," he said.

"At a most inconsiderate moment," Mr. Ricardo replied. He had been in the middle of a story, and he was not pleased.

"I'll replace it at once, sir."

"Do so, Thomson."

Thomson set the glowing lamp in the middle of the table and withdrew.

Mr. Middleton leaned forward toward Ricardo. "You

had reached the point where you tiptoed down the stairs—"

"No, no," Ricardo interrupted. "The chain is broken. The savor of the story gone. It was a poor story, anyway."

"You mustn't say that," cried Hanaud. "The story was of a thrill. The Miss Braddon at her best."

"Oh, well, well, if you really think so," said Mr. Ricardo, tittering modestly.

The three faces smiled contentedly in the light of the lamp, when suddenly Hanaud uttered a cry. "Look! Look!"

It was a cry so sharp that the other two men were captured by it and had to look where Hanaud was looking. The Ginger King was staring at the lamp, its amber eyes as red as the flame in the globe, its body trembling. They saw it rise onto its feet and leap onto the edge of the table, where it crouched again and rose again, its eyes never changing from their direction. Very delicately it padded between the silver ornaments across the shining mahogany. Then it sat back upon its haunches and, raising its forepaws, struck once violently at the globe of the lamp. The blow was so swift, so savage that it shocked the three men who watched. The lamp crashed upon the table with a sound of broken glass, and the burning oil ran this way and that, dropping in great gouts of fire onto the carpet.

Middleton and Ricardo sprang up; a chair was overturned.

"We'll have the whole house on fire," cried Ricardo, as he rang the bell in a panic. Hanaud had just time to snatch up the cat as it dived at the green cloth on the base of the stand, before the flames caught it. It screamed and fought and clawed like a mad thing. To get away? No, to get back to the overturned lamp.

The Ginger King

Already there was a smell of burning fabrics in the room. Some dried feathery grass in a vase caught a sprinkle of the burning oil and flamed up against the wallpaper. Thomson arrived with all the rugs he could hurriedly gather to smother the fire. Pails of water were brought, but a good many minutes passed before the conflagration was extinguished and the four men, with their clothes disheveled and their hands and faces begrimed, could look around upon the ruin of the room.

"I should have guessed," said Hanaud remorsefully. "The Unicorn Company saves its twenty-five thousand pounds. Yes, but Mr. Ricardo's fine dining room will need a good deal of restoration."

Later on that night, in a smaller room, when the electric light was burning and the three men were washed and refreshed, Hanaud made his apology.

"I asked you, Mr. Middleton, inside the burned walls of the house in Berwick Street whether it was lit with electric light. And you answered, 'with that and with nothing else.' But I had seen a broken oil lamp among the litter. I suspected that lamp, but the house was empty for an hour and a half before the fire broke out. I couldn't get over that fact. Then I smelled something, something acrid—just a whiff of it. It came from a broken bottle lying by the bath with other broken bottles and a broken glass shelf, such as a man has in his bathroom to hold his little medicines, his toothpaste, his shaving soap. I put the broken bottle in my pocket, and a little of that pungent smell clung to my fingers.

"At the police station at once the cat made friends with

me. Why? I did not guess. In fact, I flattered myself a little. I say, 'Hanaud, animals love you.' But it was not so. The Ginger King loved my smelly fingers, that was all. Then came the strange behavior of Enoch Swallow. Cats made him physically sick. Yet this one he must take away before it could betray him. He could not carry it under his coat. No, that was too much. But he could go out and buy a basket—and without any fear. Do you remember how cunningly he looked around the office and up at the ceiling, and how satisfied he was to leave the cat with us. Why? I noticed the look, but I could not understand it. It was because all the lights in the room were bulbs hanging from the ceiling. There was not a standing lamp anywhere. Afterward I get the cat. I drive to the chemist, leaving the cat in its basket in the cab.

"I pull out my broken bottle, and I ask the chemist. 'What is it that was in this bottle?'

"He smells and he says at once, 'Valerian.'

"I say, 'What is valerian?'

"He answers, 'Valerian has a volatile oil that when exposed to the air develops a pungent and unpleasant smell. It is used for hysteria, insomnia, and nervous ailments.'

"That does not help me, but I draw a target at a venture. I ask, 'Has it anything to do with cats?'

"The assistant, he looks at me as if I was off my rocker and he says, 'It drives them mad, that's all.' And at once I say, 'Give me some!' At this point, Hanaud fetched out of his pocket a bottle of tincture of valerian.

"I have this—yes. But I am still a little stupid. I do not connect the broken lamp and the valerian and the Ginger King—no, not until I see him step up with his eyes all mad and on fire onto the mahogany table. And then it is too late.

"You see, the good Enoch practiced a little first. He smears the valerian on the base of the lamp, and he teaches the cat to knock it over to get at the valerian. Then one night he shuts the cat up in some thin linen bag through which in time it can claw its freedom. He smears the base of the lamp with valerian, lights it, and goes off to the cinema.

"The house is empty—yes. But the cat is there in the bag, and the lamp is lit, and every minute the valerian at the bottom of the lamp smells more and more. And more and more the cat is maddened. Tonight there was no valerian on the lamp, but the Ginger King, he knows that that is where valerian is to be found. I shall find out when I get back to Paris whether there was any trace of a burned cat at the fire on the Boulevard Haussmann.

"But"—and he turned toward Mr. Middleton—"you will keep the Ginger King that he may repeat his performance at the Courts of Law, and you will not pay one brass bean to that honest peasant from Syria."

My Boss the Cat

PAUL GALLICO

If you are thinking of acquiring a cat at your house and would care for a quick sketch of what your life will be like under *Felis domesticus*, you have come to the right party. I have figured out that, to date, I have worked for—and I mean *worked for*—thirty-nine of these four-legged characters, including one memorable period when I was doing the bidding of some twenty-three assorted resident felines all at the same time.

Cats are, of course, no good. They're chiselers and panhandlers, sharpers and shameless flatterers. They're as full of schemes and plans, plots and counterplots, wiles and guiles as any confidence man. They can read your character better than a fifty-dollar-an-hour psychiatrist. They know to a milligram how much of the old oil to pour on to break you down. They are definitely smarter than I am, which is one reason why I love 'em.

Cat haters will try to floor you with the old argument, "If cats are so smart, why can't they do tricks, the way dogs do?" It isn't that cats can't do tricks; it's that they *won't*. They're far too hep to stand up and beg for food when they know in advance you'll give it to them anyway. And as for rolling over or playing dead or "speaking," what's in it for pussy that isn't already hers?

Cats, incidentally, are a great warm-up for a successful marriage; they teach you your place in the household. The first thing Kitty does is to organize your home on a comfortable basis—*her* basis. She'll eat when she wants to; she'll go out at her pleasure. She'll come in when she gets good and ready, if at all.

She wants attention when she wants it and darned well means to be let alone when she has other things on her mind. She is jealous; she won't have you showering attentions or caresses on any other minxes, whether two- or four-footed.

She gets upset when you come home late and when you go away on a business trip. But when *she* decides to stay out a couple of nights, it is none of your darned business where she's been or what she's been up to. Either you trust her or you don't.

She hates dirt, bad smells, poor food, loud noises, and people you bring home unexpectedly to dinner.

89

Kitty also has her share of small-child obstinacy. She enjoys seeing you flustered, fussed, red in the face, and losing your temper. Sometimes, as she hangs about watching, you get the feeling that it is all she can do to keep from busting out laughing. And she's got the darndest knack for putting the entire responsibility for everything on *you*.

For instance, Kitty pretends that she can neither talk nor understand you and that she is therefore nothing but a poor helpless dumb animal. What a laugh! Any self-respecting racket-working cat can make you understand at all times exactly what she wants. She has one voice for "Let's eat," another for wanting out, still a third for "You don't happen to have seen my toy mouse around here, the one with the tail chewed off?" and a host of other easily identifiable speeches. She can also understand you perfectly, if she thinks there's profit in it.

I once had a cat I suspected of being able to read. This was a gent named Morris, a big tabby with topaz eyes who lived with me when I was batching it in a New York apartment. One day I had just finished writing to a lady who at that time was the object of my devotion. Naturally I brought considerable of the writer's art into telling her this. I was called to the telephone for a few minutes. When I returned, Morris was sitting on my desk reading the letter. At least, he was staring down at it, looking a little ill. He gave me that long, baffled look of which cats are capable and immediately meowed to be let out. He didn't come back for three days. Thereafter, I kept my private correspondence locked up.

The incident reminds me of another highly discriminating cat I had down on the farm by the name of Tante Hedwig. One Sunday a guest asked me whether I could make a cocktail called a Mexican.

I said I thought I could and proceeded to blend a horror of gin, pineapple juice, vermouth, bitters, and other ill-assorted ingredients. Pouring out a trial glass, I spilled it on the grass. Tante Hedwig came over, sniffed, and, with a look of shameful embarrassment, solicitously covered it over. Everybody agreed later that she had something there.

Let me warn you not to put too much stock in the theory that animals do not think and that they act only by instinct. Did you ever try to keep a cat out that wanted to come in, or vice versa? I once locked a cat in the cellar. He climbed a straight, smooth cement wall, hung on with his paws (I saw the claw marks to prove it), unfastened the window hook with his nose, and climbed out.

Cats have fabulous memories, I maintain, and also the ability to measure and evaluate what they remember. Take, for instance, our two Ukrainian grays, Chin and Chilla. My wife brought them up on a medicine dropper. We gave them love and care and a good home on a farm in New Jersey.

Eventually we had to travel abroad, so Chin and Chilla went to live with friends in Glenview, Illinois, a pretty snazzy place. Back in the United States, we went out to spend Thanksgiving in Glenview. We looked forward, among other things, to seeing our two cats. When we arrived at the house, Chin and Chilla were squatting at the top of a broad flight of stairs. As we called up a tender greeting to them, we saw an expression of horror come over both their faces. "Great heavens! It's those *paupers!*

Run!" With that, they vanished and could not be found for five hours. They were frightened to death we had come to take them back to the squalor of a country estate in New Jersey and deprive them of a room of their own in Illinois, with glassed-in sun porch, screens for their toilets, and similar super-luxuries.

After a time they made a grudging appearance and consented to play the old games and talk over old times, guardedly. But when the hour arrived for our departure, they vanished once more. Our hostess wrote us that apparently they got hold of a timetable somewhere and waited until our train was past Elkhart before coming out.

It was this same Chilla who, one day on the farm after our big ginger cat, Wuzzy, had been missing for forty-eight hours, led us to where he was, a half mile away, out of sight and out of hearing, caught in a trap. Every so often Chilla would look back to see if we were coming. Old Wuz was half dead when we got there, but when he saw Chilla he started to purr.

Two-Timing, or Leading the Double Life, is something you may be called upon to face with your cat. It means simply that Kitty manages to divide her time between two homes sufficiently far apart that each homeowner thinks she is his.

I discovered this when trying to check up on the unaccountable absences of Lulu II, a seal-point Siamese. I finally located her at the other end of the bay, mooching on an amiable spinster. When I said, "Oh, I hope that my Lulu hasn't been imposing on you," she replied indignantly, "*Your* Lulu! You mean *our* dear little Pitipoo! We've been wondering where she went when she disappeared occasionally. We do hope she hasn't been annoying *you*."

The shocking part of this story, of course, is that, for the sake of a handout, Lulu, with a pedigree as long as your arm, was willing to submit to being called Pitipoo.

Of all things a smart cat does to whip you into line, the gift of the captured mouse is the cleverest and most touching. There was Limpy, the wild barn cat down on the farm who lived off what she caught in the fields. We were already supporting four cats, but in the winter, when we went to town, we brought her along.

We had not been inside the apartment ten minutes before Limpy caught a mouse, or probably *the* mouse, and at once brought it over and laid it at our feet. Now, as indicated before, Limpy had hunted to survive. To Limpy, a dead mouse was Big and Little Casino, touchdown, home run, and Grand Slam. Yet this one she gave to us.

How can you mark it up except as rent or thanks or "Here, looka; this is the most important thing I do. You take it because I like you"? You can teach a dog to retrieve and bring you game, but only a cat will voluntarily hand over its kill to you as an unsolicited gift.

How come Kitty acts not like the beast of prey she is but like a better-class human being? I don't know the answer. The point is, she does it and makes you her slave ever after. Once you have been presented with a mouse by your cat, you will never be the same again. She can use you for a doormat. And she will, too.

The Luck of the Cat

ELIZABETH GOUDGE

What was needed, thought Ivy, as she blackleaded Miss Macallister's sitting-room grate on a cold, foggy Saturday morning, was a bit of luck. Miss Macallister, who kept lodgings in one of the gloomiest streets in London, never had any and neither did Ivy, her maid of all work, nor old Mr. Partridge who did crossword puzzles on the first floor, nor young Miss Pirbright who typed on the second floor, and least of all poor Mr. Perkins who painted in the attic. They were unfortunate, that was what it was, and through no fault of their own. They were a hard-working and virtuous lot, but all of them, it seemed, had been born on a wet Friday. Hard, thought Ivy, that facts over which one had no control, such as the day of the week one was born on, could so influence one's fate. Had she only been born on a fine Sunday she would have had a sylphlike figure, an aureole of golden hair, and a dimple, and Bert Norris in the next street, who drove a taxi and made a good thing out of it, might have removed his head from the inside of his defective engine when she passed down the street of an early morning and said a little more to her than his usual careless, "Fine day, miss," when it wasn't.

Ivy finished the grate, laid sticks and paper in readiness for the fire that Miss Macallister would have that evening if she felt she could afford it, and getting up from her knees regarded herself in the cracked mirror over the mantelpiece, noting gloomily that she looked more of a Friday's child than ever. She was short and roundabout, and her dark hair was completely and agonizedly straight. Her complexion, owing to life in a back street and a perpetual cold in the head, was not what it might have been, and she had lost a front tooth. Only her eyes were arresting, wide-open brown eyes with yellow lights in them, the eyes of an optimist.

Suddenly Ivy laughed, flinging back her head as a young colt does when it takes its first gallop. Her morning pessimism, born of getting up at six o'clock on a bitter, cold, foggy morning, was always short-lived, and the moment when her natural joy in life suddenly conquered it was a moment of exhilaration for her. As she hurled the grate brushes and the blacklead into a cupboard she was humming "One Night of Love" under her breath a semitone flat, and when she went into the backyard to empty the ashes she was singing it a whole tone flat at the top of her voice.

It was while she was emptying the ashes that the miracle happened. A noiseless dark shape slipped like a shadow out of the fog and inserted itself between Ivy's legs. It was soft as velvet, black as night, and mysterious as destiny. It was a small black cat.

"My!" said Ivy, and picked it up.

It was as wet as a drowned rat, its skeleton showed through its fur, and it had an ugly ridge around its neck, as though a rope had been tied around it. Yet it was beautiful. Its face was delicately shaped, its ears were pointed like a fawn's, and its eyes were bright green and extremely wicked.

To Ivy the wet fur and the scarred neck told a tale. "Someone's tried to drown you," she said to the cat. "Born on a wet Friday, you were."

The cat purred, closing its eyes and simpering and laying an affectionate paw on Ivy's shoulder. Its head might be, metaphorically speaking, bloody, but it was unbowed, and to show its fighting spirit it suddenly shot out the claws of its affectionate paw and stuck them into Ivy hard.

"Here, none of that!" said Ivy, and slapped it.

The cat purred on, its eyes narrowed to wicked green slits and its tail dripping dirty water all down the front of Ivy's clean apron.

But Ivy did not care for she had suddenly remembered

that a black cat brings luck. With eyes like stars she
dashed with it into the scullery, where she rubbed it dry
with a clean duster and gave it a cod's head left over from
yesterday's dinner, the mouse out of the mousetrap, and
the milk intended for the lodgers' rice puddings.

The cat ate, daintily but with greed, and Ivy watched
it, her heart pounding with excitement.

For she was nothing if not superstitious. She would
sooner have died than passed under a ladder without wishing, and if she spilled the salt she threw a pinch over her
shoulder without a moment's pause. She searched for
strangers in her teacup and knocked on wood so often that
the knuckles of her right hand were quite worn. And a
black cat! A black cat coming into their backyard entirely
on its own initiative! Ivy refilled the saucer and passed a
hand lovingly over the damp, black back.

At this moment Miss Macallister returned from upstairs, where she had been interviewing the lodgers about
their dinners and making her usual daily suggestion of "a
nice rice pudding and a few stewed prunes for a change."

"Where did that cat come from?" she demanded sharply,
her gaunt figure rigid in horror and her gray eyes fixed
and staring behind their steel-rimmed glasses.

"It just walked in, ma'am," triumphed Ivy. "It means
luck, ma'am, luck for us all."

"Is that," asked Miss Macallister, faintly but icily, "the
lodgers' milk?"

"Yes, ma'am," said Ivy belligerently. "The poor creature's 'alf-starved, and it's 'ad the lot."

Miss Macallister was not an unkind woman, indeed she
was quite the reverse, harboring out of sheer pity lodgers

who paid their bills erratically and stinting herself rather than Ivy when food was short, but she could not afford cats who imbibed the lodgers' milk.

"Ivy," she said, "take that cat through the yard and shut it out in the street. I won't have it here. I can't afford it."

Ivy glared at her employer, and her employer glared at her. Miss Macallister's tall, black-clad figure, topped with a chignon of gray hair, seemed made of iron and steel, and Ivy knew she was momentarily beaten. When the old girl turned hard like that, there was no doing anything with her. She obediently picked up the cat and marched with it through the yard and out into the back street beyond, closing the yard door behind her with a bang.

Miss Macallister sighed with relief. She had feared one of those battle royals that she sometimes had with Ivy, battles rendered all the harder for both of them by the fact that they were secretly devoted to each other. But the child was a good child and amenable to reason.

But Ivy was not being quite as good as Miss Macallister thought. Once out in the street, with the yard door banged behind her, she held up the cat by the scruff of its neck and addressed it in language almost fierce in its intensity.

"Now look 'ere," she said, "I'm not going to chuck you out to be drowned and lose the luck of the 'ole 'ouse along with you. I'm going to keep you." She shook the cat slightly, to give point to her remarks. "I'll keep you, but I'll 'ave to keep you 'idden. And you'll 'ave to back me up, mind. No squeaking now, when the old girl's about, and no walking out of places what I've 'id you in. Is that a bargain, Black Sambo?"

Green eyes and hazel eyes met in an unwinking regard,

and the bargain was ratified. Ivy removed the bib of her apron, always secured in place by a large steel safety pin, unfastened her print dress, which opened down the front and was kept together by two pins and a darning needle, and placed Sambo in her bosom. He was very small, and when the dress and the voluminous bib were repinned over him, you could hardly have told, in the dim, foggy light, that he was there at all.

Ivy returned to the kitchen looking as though butter would not melt in her mouth. "Shall I clear the lodgers' breakfasts, ma'am?" she inquired sweetly.

"You're a good girl, Ivy," said Miss Macallister, and laid her hand, with an unusual gesture of affection, on the girl's shoulder. Ivy responded with one of her quick, warm smiles. She stood like a dancer, half turned away from Miss Macallister and looking up over her shoulder, so that her front was hidden. A curious attitude, Miss Macallister thought, but becoming to her.

It always took Ivy a good long while to clear the breakfasts because she had to stop and chat with each of the lodgers in turn. Miss Macallister never complained of the time she took, for she thought it probable that the presence of Ivy acted on the lodgers as it did on her—as a tonic.

"Good morning, Mr. Partridge," said Ivy cheerily, as she entered the first-floor front room with her tin tray held well in front of her and the bib of her apron rippling curiously.

Mr. Partridge, his newspaper on the floor beside him, was sitting crouched over his gas fire, his blue-veined old hands held out to its warmth and his dressing gown draped over his shabby tweed coat to keep the fog away from his lumbago. His bald head looked bonier than ever, Ivy thought, and his straggly gray beard stragglier. He had kept a grocer's shop in his day, but he hadn't done well with it and was thankful now for the old-age pension that provided him with rice pudding and prunes and a roof over his head. Though he would have liked something more. The wireless that he longed for, and a few comforts, and the wherewithal to do a good turn to other people now and again. For years he had been doing the Saturday crossword puzzle in the *Weekly Chronicle*, which offered fifty pounds to the winner, but there always seemed to be some silly little thing that he got wrong, or else, if he was right for once, he wasn't pulled out first. There was some trick about these things, he felt. It was difficult not to be discouraged.

Ivy halted in astonishment when she saw Mr. Partridge's *Weekly Chronicle* on the floor, for on a Saturday morning she was accustomed to seeing him holding it eagerly in front of his nose and to having shot at her such inane questions as, "Can you think, Ivy, of a word of nine letters for a trousered character in Italian comedy? It ends with an *e*, Ivy dear." To which she would reply, never having heard of the word *pantalone*, "I couldn't say, Mr. Partridge, I'm sure. Miss Macallister wants to know, sir, if you'd fancy a nice bit of boiled cod today? They're out of tripe."

"Why, Mr. Partridge, sir!" she cried this morning. "Why aren't you doing your crossword?"

Mr. Partridge shook his head sadly. "It's no good, Ivy," he mourned. "They never pull me out first. There's some trick. I shan't do any more crosswords."

The Luck of the Cat

Ivy set her tray down on the table with a bang and planted herself in front of Mr. Partridge on the rag hearthrug. If the old fellow gave up doing his crosswords, she might as well go out and order his hearse for Friday week straight away, and so save trouble later, for they were his one link with life. "Here, none of that!" she said severely, as she had said to the cat when she slapped it for its good, and picking up the paper and folding it back at the crossword puzzle she laid it firmly on his knee.

But Mr. Partridge made no effort to take it and it slipped off again.

"My!" said Ivy. "You're in a poor way, you are. Now just you look here."

She removed the safety pin, the darning needle, and the two pins, and she pulled Sambo out from his hiding place, holding the handful of black fur and the wicked green eyes in front of the astonished old man. "That walked in this morning," she continued. "Honor bright it did. Walked straight in. It means luck, Mr. Partridge, luck for us all, so just you get on with that puzzle. Oh, and there'll be no rice pudding today, the cat's had the milk, only prunes. Oh, and, Mr. Partridge, don't you tell the old girl about Sambo, for she told me to throw 'im out and she thinks I 'ave. As if I'd throw away a handful of luck like this! Oh, and, Mr. Partridge, any bits of food you could manage to keep back from your meals for 'im, a bloater tail or anything like that, I'd be truly grateful."

Mr. Partridge nodded, but he still made no move to pick up his paper. "It's all superstition, Ivy," he said gloomily. "Black cats don't bring luck. I had three black cats at one time, and it didn't do me any good. But it's a nice cat," he added, and he stretched out a horny finger and rubbed Sambo behind his beautiful pointed ears. Sambo purred with great suddenness and lifted his delicate chin that he might be rubbed beneath that too. He had under it, hitherto unnoticed by Ivy, a little white spot the size of a threepenny bit. Truly an attractive cat.

When Ivy had gone Mr. Partridge reached absently for his paper. Ivy and Sambo had cheered him up, and his unconscious reaction was to do the usual thing. He lifted the paper and adjusted his glasses, looking at it where Ivy had folded it.

"A carnivorous quadruped given to visual activity near the throne and in former times worshipped by the Egyptians."

Mr. Partridge was instantly alert for this was just the sort of cue that he delighted in, calling as it did for considerable intellectual effort and historical knowledge. "One across. Four letters," he murmured. "I know! Ibis. That's an animal the Egyptians worshipped." He eagerly fetched his dictionary, but the wretched creature turned out to be a kind of stork. By no stretch of imagination could it be called a carnivorous quadruped. Mr. Partridge was cast down, but brightened again. "Got it!" he said. "Lion. A royal animal."

But lion didn't seem to fit, for one down was a disease of nine letters from which infants suffer, and try as he might Mr. Partridge couldn't think of anything that fitted the case except paralysis. "P," said Mr. Partridge. "Pork. Pony. Pug." And then it suddenly came to him. "Puss!" A cat may look at a king, and the Egyptians, a sensible people, had the wisdom to bow the knee to that mysterious, beautiful, aloof, uncanny creature we call a cat.

The Luck of the Cat

After that Mr. Partridge found the rest of the puzzle easy. He worked at it all morning, his mind illumined by a clarity he had not known for years and his eyes alight like those of a child.

Ivy meanwhile, having removed the bones of Mr. Partridge's haddock to the kitchen, journeyed on to Miss Pirbright's sitting room on the second floor. Miss Pirbright was a very humble journalist on the staff of a cheap daily paper. Every afternoon and evening she scurried about London collecting material for the gossip column, and every morning she typed what she hoped were bright snappy little bits calculated to save her from the sack. She was twenty, with curly dark hair and appealing brown eyes, and she would have been pretty had her life not been clouded by anxiety and unrequited love. Fear of the sack had dimmed her eyes and bowed her shoulders, and love for Mr. Perkins in the attic kept her awake at night and made it quite impossible for her to digest Miss Macallister's insufficiently stewed prunes.

Ivy was continually trying to build up her morale by repeating to her the aphorisms that kept Ivy herself going. "Never cross your bridges until you get to 'em," she would say, as she emptied the slops, and "Don't worry it may not 'appen," and "There are as good fish in the sea as ever came out of it," and "Take no thought for the morrow," and, with an upward jerk of the head toward Mr. Perkins' attic, "Everything comes to 'er what waits."

But none of it seemed to do Miss Pirbright any good. She remained hopelessly pessimistic.

This morning Ivy found her dejectedly cleaning her

typewriter and so depressed that she did not even look up until Ivy hung Sambo around her neck from behind, after the style of a feather boa. She screamed and leaped to her feet, and then, seeing what it was that draped her shoulders and stuck pins into her, cried out in ecstasy, "A black cat! Ivy! A black cat!"

"Luck," said Ivy, and Sambo, his head against Miss Pirbright's left ear, purred loudly.

But at this Miss Pirbright shook her head. "That's only superstition, Ivy," she said, as she rubbed her cheek against Sambo's soft fur.

"Is it!" said Ivy. "You wait. And will you please keep bits of your bloaters and 'addocks for 'im? And will you please not tell Miss Macallister that 'e is resident in the 'ouse?"

Miss Pirbright promised, and Ivy, having repinned Sambo and removed the remains of Miss Pirbright's breakfast, departed.

But Miss Pirbright did not immediately return to the cleaning of her typewriter. Instead, she pulled a suitcase out from under her bed and abstracted from it a bundle of typescript tied up in brown paper. It was a novel she had written, and a fortnight ago, when it had come home to roost with its sixth rejection slip, she had vowed she would never send it out again.

But this morning, somehow, she felt differently about it. She could still feel the soft touch of fur on her neck and hear a cheerful humming in her ear, and it made her feel different. Sitting back on her heels on the floor, she flicked over a few pages, reading bits here and there, and the book seemed to her a good deal less bad than it had done the last time she dipped into it. "At least it's better than most of the rubbish they publish nowadays," said Miss Pirbright to herself. "I'll send it out once more. Just once more." She was not, of course, she told herself, in the least influenced by Ivy's nonsense about a black cat bringing luck; it was just that she felt unaccountably cheered up and hopeful.

She fetched paper and string, packed it up and addressed it to the seventh publisher, and hurried out with it at once to the nearest post office without giving herself time to change her mind. When she came back again, she had color in her cheeks and a sparkle in her eyes after her run in the cold air, and when she began her typing, there was some magic in her fingers that made the sound of the little tapping hammers sound more like gnomes jubilantly step dancing on a crystal floor than the tin bucket falling downstairs to which Mr. Perkins upstairs usually irritably compared it.

He was more irritable than ever when Ivy entered to remove the dried haddock—and the haddocks meted out by Miss Macallister to lodgers who didn't pay their bills were always very dry indeed—that he hadn't even touched.

"I can't, Ivy," he said, indicating it with the stem of his pipe. "I can't get the damn thing down. I tell you it is not fit for human food. It is blotting paper coated with glue."

"Go on!" said Ivy. "Don't talk nonsense. If you can't fancy good food, I know who can," and she unpinned her front.

Instantly a delicately curved black shape executed a

graceful pirouette in the air and landed on the haddock. With amazing rapidity it absorbed the haddock, and presently nothing was left on the dish but a network of bones clean and dainty as a spider's web.

Mr. Perkins threw back his head and laughed, the first genuine laugh he had perpetrated for more than a month. Then he picked up Sambo by his scruff and looked at him. Sambo looked back out of his unblinking green eyes, carefully wiping his whiskers with his tongue as he did so.

"Luck," said Ivy firmly. "Luck for you, Mr. Perkins."

"Likely!" ejaculated Mr. Perkins, and dropping Sambo with heartless suddenness he swung savagely around and glared at the cold, unlit gas fire. It was one of those irritating shilling-in-the-slot things and had just died on him. He didn't have another shilling.

He was twenty-six, with a tall, lanky figure, a fair, pointed beard, a brown velveteen jacket, and a blue bow tie with flowing ends that had matched his eyes when it was new but didn't now that he had spilled a good deal of egg over it. Miss Pirbright thought he looked extraordinarily artistic and distinguished, but Ivy, though she liked him, thought he looked a perfect idiot. Miss Pirbright always named him Adonis in her thoughts and Ivy the Attic. He painted pictures of which it was impossible to say whether they were right way up or wrong way up. They were very clever, but still for the most part unbought.

That very morning Mr. Perkins had come to the conclusion that he would paint no more pictures. The little attic with a north light, beyond his bed sitting room, which he used for a studio, was already almost entirely blocked by canvases. Of what use, he had asked himself, to block the room entirely up so that he couldn't even move in it? And of what use to produce scores of masterpieces for which the world, as devoid of taste as of common sense in this twentieth century, had no use? Before Ivy brought his breakfast up he had practically decided to take to the road and become a tramp, and the sight of the everlasting breakfast haddock, and the thought of the everlasting prunes and rice that would in due course follow, had decided him. If one slept at a different workhouse each night, there was bound to be a certain amount of variety in the menus.

"I shall chuck painting, Ivy," he announced, swinging around. "I have painted my last picture, I shall—"

And then he stopped dead, his jaw dropping and his eyes widening, transfixed by the picture he saw in front of him.

A sudden gleam of sun had conquered the fog and was lighting up Ivy where she stood with Sambo in her arms, her chin resting on top of his head. It did not spare the blemishes of either of them; the pimples on Ivy's sallow skin, her work-reddened hands, the ugly bones that showed through Sambo's fur, his scarred neck were very noticeable. But it also illumined their beauties in a rather startling way. Ivy's eyes, fixed thoughtfully on Mr. Perkins and alight with tolerant amusement, were just the color of a certain stream that he knew, one of those brown New Forest streams where the water is so sparkling and clear that every pebble below is shown shining like a jewel, as deliciously visible as were the thoughts behind Ivy's eyes— her honest, courageous, kindly thoughts. Her broad, ugly mouth was lifted a little at each corner and her lips were just parted, as though a laugh had laid a hand upon the latch and was just about to walk in. "And lips, oh you the doors of breath," murmured Mr. Perkins to himself, but he did not say it aloud because quotations from the poets annoyed Ivy and he did not want to disturb the exquisite laughing tenderness of her expression.

And Sambo. Under her chin his triangular face had the velvety softness of a pansy, and his great eyes were alight with the pagan fire of his race. His ears, shaped like flower petals, tapering to almost invisible points and cheekily cocked, were exquisite, and the paws hanging over Ivy's wrists were in repose deliciously rounded.

And the picture was not devoid of color. The sudden beam of sun lighted like a pointed finger on Ivy's blueprint dress and Sambo's rich, black fur against her white apron. It lit golden lights in Ivy's brown eyes and turned Sambo's to blazing emeralds. It even laid a caressing hand on Ivy's ugly hair and illumined Sambo's whiskers so that they showed like horizontal threads of silver.

Mr. Perkins looked long and earnestly and then dashed into his studio and slammed the door.

"He's dotty," declared Ivy, and cleared away his breakfast.

In his studio Mr. Perkins set up a fresh canvas on his easel, squeezed paint onto his palette with feverish haste, and began. Later, of course, he would have to get Ivy and Sambo to sit for him, but at once, while it was fresh in his mind, he must get down the chief notes of color: the blue and sharp black and white, the gold and green and silver. And above all he must get while he remembered it the look in Ivy's eyes, the laugh knocking at her lips, and the cat's look of poised, attentive naughtiness.

As he worked he became conscious of a delightful tapping sound. He was too busy to identify it, but he found himself thinking of such delightful things as a spring shower falling on shiny beech leaves and a woodpecker tapping on the bark of a walnut tree. His thoughts were not without effect on his painting. The gaiety of the spring crept into it, and the cleanliness of the falling rain. And he was aware, too, of a sense of clarity that came to him from somewhere beyond the tapping sound and that seemed to pervade the house, as though its atmosphere had freshened. That also affected his work and gave it a certain simplicity, so that by lunchtime the least artistic observer would have been able to say which way up the picture was intended to be looked at.

One o'clock struck.

Miss Pirbright lifted her cramped fingers from her typewriter and gave a little laugh. She actually was looking forward to a dinner of boiled cod and stewed prunes.

Could it be one already? thought old Mr. Partridge. The morning had flown. Well, he could swear that he had done an extraordinarily difficult crossword absolutely correctly, and yet his mind was quite unexhausted; that wonderful clearness of brain was with him still. And there was Ivy coming up the stairs with that delicious cod.

Mr. Perkins, though he distinctly heard his cod dumped on the table in the next room, took no notice. He painted on and on.

* * *

On an afternoon a few weeks later Mr. Perkins stood waiting in the library of a house in the West End. He was clutching his dilapidated green felt hat in his hands and remembering that he ought to have left it in the hall. Beads of perspiration stood on his forehead for he was both tired and hot after walking so many miles carrying his picture of Ivy and Sambo under his arm. It stood against a chair near him, in the very lovely frame that had been paid for by old Mr. Partridge out of the money he had most astonishingly won for the correct solution of a crossword puzzle, pulled out first.

All around him, reaching apparently to infinity, stretched the beauty of the library—its soft pile carpet and velvet curtains, its thousand books, its furniture and chairs and priceless pictures.

It was these last that had unnerved poor Mr. Perkins. How had he dared to bring his paltry little picture to the house of a man who owned masterpieces like these? How would he, when that man opened the door and walked in, dare to ask him to buy it? He reminded himself that Conrad Myers, a noted patron of the arts, was particularly fond of modern pictures and that many of his fellow-artists of the modern school had succeeded in selling their work to him. But that did not cheer him up much for he was not one of his fellow-artists, he was himself, and never before had he so humiliated that self as to beg from a private individual in this way. In the past he had sold his work to dealers or not at all. It had been mostly not at all, but at least he had kept his self-respect.

It was that confounded black cat, he told himself, who had fooled him. Ivy's ridiculous faith in the luck it was bringing them all had influenced him in spite of himself, so that he had really thought his picture a little master-piece, worthy of being offered to Conrad Myers.

The door opened and that worthy came in, a tall man whose tight-lipped face was without kindness, and at sight of him any sense that might previously have been left in Mr. Perkins' head immediately left it.

Isolated sentences of their conversation seemed to come to him from a long way off as he and Conrad Myers backed away from the picture to see its general effect, drew nearer to it to see its detail, gamboled sideways to get the light on it and in circles to test its general merit.

"No," said the great man. "Old-fashioned. I am an admirer of modern work. Whoever told you to bring that rubbish to me?"

"But I *am* modern," gasped Mr. Perkins, wiping his forehead with the back of his hand.

"Modern?" said Mr. Myers. "That?"

Mr. Perkins looked at his picture again and realized with a shock of surprise that the criticism was a true one. It *was* old-fashioned. For the first time he saw it as it really was, and the sight appalled him. It might, he thought savagely, have appeared upon the outside of the Christmas Number of *The Sphere*. He had painted it as a child paints, laying on bright colors lavishly and gaily, all his carefully acquired theories on the subject of composition, restraint, and color value apparently scattered to the winds. Moreover, it was painfully obvious—you could tell what the subject was a mile off—and it was sentimental, a poor girl with a cat in her arms, her motherly face against its fur. What could be worse?

Like one in a dream, Mr. Perkins suffered himself to be told what Mr. Myers thought of him, to be handed over to a pompous ass of a butler, to be placed in a taxi with his wretched picture and dismissed from the West End in deserved contumely. And this was his expected luck!

It was only when the taxi had turned several corners that he realized he had no money to pay for it. "Hi!" he yelled, and rapped on the glass.

The taxi came to rest in the gutter, and a nice young driver with cheerful red hair came around to him. "Yes, sir?"

"I was trying to sell a picture at that house, and the fool of a butler called a taxi for me that I can't afford. I haven't a bean. I'm awfully sorry. You must let me get out."

The young taxi driver took it well. "Right you are, sir," he said genially, and opened the door, revealing the picture. "'Ere!" he ejaculated suddenly, forgetting his manners. "If that ain't Ivy Baker!"

"It is," said Mr. Perkins. "Have you the good fortune to know the lady?"

"I live in the next street," said the driver in a burst of confidence. "Bert Norris my name is. Yes, I know Ivy. Whatever made you paint 'er? She's no beauty."

"Oh, isn't she?" said Mr. Perkins. "You look again."

Bert looked again. The spring sunshine fell upon Ivy, doing full justice to her eyes and her laughing mouth and the tender, motherly expression that could not fail to move one who, like Bert, had not had the springs of sentiment dried up in him by modern thought. "She ain't a bad girl," he said reflectively, scratching his jaw.

"She ain't," said Mr. Perkins. "There are few women in this world to touch Ivy. She is a remarkable woman. I lodge in the house where she works, and I know."

The Luck of the Cat

"Pity you couldn't sell the picture," said Bert.

"I didn't deserve to," said Mr. Perkins. "It's a good likeness of Ivy, but it's a rotten bad picture. It's the sort of rubbish they put in the Academy."

"'Ave yer tried the Academy?" inquired Bert.

"What?" gasped Mr. Perkins.

"They're judgin' pictures for the spring show now," said Bert. "I've been all the morning carting artistic blokes there with their pictures, and all of 'em was a lot worse than what yours is. I'll drive you around there now, and you can pay me at your convenience."

For a minute or two Mr. Perkins, still sitting in the taxi, thought hard. For years he had considered the Academy infinitely beneath him—but yet—if a picture exhibited in it attracted attention, orders came thick and fast. And, of course, if men such as himself, with really advanced and intellectual ideas about art, could once succeed in getting into the Academy that institution would be very greatly benefited.

He sat back in his seat. "Drive on, Bert," he said.

It was two days after Mr. Perkins' picture had been accepted for the Academy that Miss Macallister gave a tea party to her lodgers. She had never done such a thing before, but such wonderful things had been happening to them all lately that she felt they really ought to have a little celebration.

To begin with, there was old Mr. Partridge winning fifty pounds for a crossword puzzle. It had made a new man of him, or perhaps it would be more accurate to say that the wireless he had bought had made a new man of him. He loved it as a lover his lady. He listened to it all day and as much of the night as the B.B.C. would permit, driving the rest of the house distracted with the noise he made, and his horizons had widened to take in the whole world. And he had not forgotten other people in his good fortune. Besides the frame for the famous picture, he had purchased presents for everyone else in the house, and very well-chosen and appropriate presents, too. Miss Macallister smoothed her purple silk scarf lovingly. And he had paid up the money owing to Miss Macallister from all of them.

And then there was Miss Pirbright's novel, which had been accepted by a well-known publisher. Miss Pirbright had made no money out of it as yet, but she seemed to have no doubt that she would. Personally, Miss Macallister had her doubts, though she didn't say so. After all, what really mattered to Miss Pirbright's happiness was not money that might or might not be forthcoming but the fact that Mr. Perkins had actually noticed her at last. He had been absolutely astounded that she should have had the intelligence to write a novel and, what was more, for lots of women wrote unsaleable novels, have it accepted. On the strength of it he asked her to tea in his attic and found she was quite pretty enough to take notice of. And the more he noticed her the prettier she got. And the prettier she got the more he noticed her. Nothing could have been more satisfactory.

And it was the same with Ivy and Bert. Mr. Perkins' considered opinion that Ivy was a remarkable woman had not been without influence. Bert now escorted her to the pictures weekly, refreshing her with chocolate creams all the while, and Ivy was growing quite fat.

The Luck of the Cat

With all this young love about the place Miss Macallister couldn't help feeling a little lonely. She had also been a little hurt that Mr. Perkins had not shown her his picture before he took it to the Academy. She knew it was a portrait of Ivy, but that was all she knew, and after all Ivy was her maid so surely she had a right to see the picture. He had showed it to the others but not to her. That, she thought, definitely placed her in the category of old maids who are not wanted. She couldn't help wishing that she had not, for reasons of economy, turned out that black cat. It would have been something to love. And as things had turned out, with Mr. Partridge paying up all the money owing, she could quite well have afforded to indulge herself. Well, it just showed that there was nothing in the saying that to turn away a black cat is to turn away luck, for she had turned one away and just look at the good fortune that had come to the house.

At this moment Ivy entered with the tea tray and a grand sugar cake.

"I wish, Ivy," said Miss Macallister, "that I had not turned away that black cat. I have it on my conscience."

"It's a funny thing, ma'am," said Ivy, "but I often see that cat out in the street beyond the yard. Poor little thing! It looks as though it wanted a good 'ome."

"Ivy!" cried Miss Macallister. "Run out and see if it is there now. If it is, bring it in."

Ivy ran, going rather unaccountably upstairs to fetch something first, and returning in an astonishingly short space of time with an armful of black fur that she dumped on Miss Macallister's lap.

"The beauty!" cried Miss Macallister, stroking and

petting. "The beauty! But how fat he's got, Ivy, since I saw him last."

"It's just his thick fur," explained Ivy, laying the tea. "When you saw him last, he was wet."

"See how he likes me, Ivy," said Miss Macallister, as Sambo, playing up and purring loudly, revolved on her lap, kneading her with his paws so as to make of her a satisfactory surface on which to repose.

He was comfortably settled when the guests arrived. He showed no signs of recognition, indeed he stared at them with the greatest insolence, quite as though he and the remains of their bloaters and haddocks had never been acquainted, and they, on receiving winks from Ivy, were overcome with astonishment at finding a cat at Miss Macallister's.

"Yes," she said with dignity. "I have decided to keep a cat. Now, Pharaoh, say how-do-you-do to the lady and gentlemen."

"Pharaoh?" faltered Miss Pirbright.

"Yes," said Miss Macallister. "An Egyptian title. A royal title. Cats, if you remember, were worshipped in ancient Egypt."

Mr. Partridge, Miss Pirbright, Mr. Perkins, and Ivy all fell upon their knees.

Royally enthroned, Pharaoh turned his head slowly from side to side, his wicked green eyes wide, his pointed ears pricked, his pansy face bland, and his claws in. Very graciously he purred encouragement while they, like the Egyptians of old, did homage.

Cat Nipped

JACK SCHAEFER

Corporal Clint Buckner ambled slowly across the flat, baked surface of what would someday be the parade ground of Fort McKay. He carried a stubby cavalry carbine in the crook of his left elbow and patted the stock affectionately with his right hand as he walked. The hot Kansas sun beat full strength upon him and upon the double row of tents that flanked one side of the level space and upon the three sod-walled structures that stretched at a right angle to mark another side. The sun beat with equal untiring fervor upon the sweating bodies of Sergeant Peattie and a crew of half-naked privates piling strips of sod one on another for the walls of the first of the structures that would line the third side.

Corporal Clint ambled in a slow curve to pass near Sergeant Peattie and his swearing crew. He paused to yawn and wipe imaginary dust from the carbine and ambled on. The dripping privates stopped their work to watch him move past.

"Ain't he the brave hunter, toting that big gun."

"Takes nerve to go after those critters like he does."

"Yep. Turrible dangerous when wounded."

Chuckles and a climbing guffaw disturbed the afternoon quiet. Corporal Clint paid no attention to them. "Envy makes a mighty strong poison," he remarked to no one in particular. He ambled on to the doorway of the middle of the three sod-walled structures and into the shaded interior.

Outside the sun beat down with steady glare. Inside Corporal Clint widened his eyes to look through the relatively cool dimness. He stood in a semblance of attention and raised his right hand in a limp salute. Angled across from him in a corner, Lieutenant Henley, acting commissary officer, was perched on a stool using an upturned packing box as a desk. Lieutenant Henley waggled a hand in what could have been a languid salute or a mere greeting and returned to pencil figuring on a piece of wrapping paper. Corporal Clint perched himself on another stool with his back to the wall where he could look along the rough ground-floored aisle between two long piles of grain in bags. He set the carbine across his knees.

Partway down the aisle between the grain bags a prairie mouse crept out and into the open and darted back and crept out again. Corporal Clint raised the carbine and aimed with casual ease and fired. There was a smudge on the ground where the mouse had been. Over in his corner Lieutenant Henley looked up. Corporal Clint nodded at him. Lieutenant Henley reached with his pencil and made a mark beside many other marks on a piece of paper tacked to the side of his box desk. He sighed and returned to his figuring. Corporal Clint took out of a pocket a linen cartridge holding its lead ball and powder and reloaded the carbine. He inspected the percussion cap. He set the carbine on his knees and watched the aisle in quiet content.

Outside the sun beat down upon the laboring soldiers. Inside was shaded silence punctured only by the occasional sharp blast of the carbine and the sighs and some soft new anguished grunts from Lieutenant Henley. Corporal Clint smiled drowsily to himself. A mouse slipped into view. Corporal Clint raised the carbine.

"Stop that infernal racket!"

Corporal Clint jumped to his feet. He snapped to attention. Off in his corner Lieutenant Henley did the same. Captain McKay stood in the doorway, mopping his face and peering into the dimness.

"How's a man to get a report written or even take a nap wondering when that damn thing's going off again?" Captain McKay waved Corporal Clint aside and sat on the stool by the wall and stretched out his legs. "An infernal nuisance."

"You're right, sir." Lieutenant Henley came forward with his paper in his hand. "And useless, sir. Utterly and completely useless."

"Yes?"

"Well, sir, I've been doing some figuring." Lieutenant

119

Henley's voice was weighty with overtones of awe. "According to that animal book, these damn mice have four to ten young ones at a time, and it only takes them six weeks to have them. Worse than that, they start breeding soon as they're six weeks old." Lieutenant Henley sighed and stared down in somber fascination at his paper. "Well, sir, you take a middle figure for that litter number to be on the safe side, and you just say only half each litter is females, and you say again only half those females live to breeding age, and all the same starting with just one pair after ten generations you've got close to half a million of those damn mice ruining my commissary, and all of them busy breeding when they're not eating, and they're averaging about a bag of grain a day already and making holes in all the bags. They're multiplying fifty times faster than Buckner here could kill them if he was triplets and every one of him as good a shot."

Captain McKay mopped his face again. "A formidable enemy, the way you put it."

"Beg pardon, sir, but it's no joke." Lieutenant Henley waggled his piece of paper. "We'll run short of feed for the horses, and they're getting into our own provisions. We could try wooden bins, but we can't get any good wood out on this damned prairie, and they'd gnaw through it anyway. I just don't know what to do."

"Cats," said Corporal Clint.

Captain McKay slumped in his chair and drummed fingers on the onetime kitchen table that was his desk. From behind the hanging canvas partition that marked off his one-room living quarters in the same sod-walled building came a soft melodic humming and other small bustling noises as his wife moved about engaged in some incomprehensible feminine activity. The humming annoyed him. Two months they had been out here on the empty prairie, creating an Army post out of next to nothing with supplies always short and no new appropriation to draw on for things needed, and he didn't even have decent quarters for her yet because he was an old-line Army fool who believed in taking good care of his men first, and still she was cheerful and could hum silly tunes and never once complain. By rights she ought to complain. And because she wouldn't, he couldn't, not even in the bosom, so to speak, of his own family and had to go on pretending to be a noble soul who enjoyed hardship for the sake of duty nobly done.

His fingers stopped drumming, and he looked down again at the canceled requisition that had been returned in the fortnightly mail. Clipped to it was a note in vigorous handwriting: "Mac, lucky I caught this before it went any higher. Cats! You're starting a post out there not a blooming menagerie. Next thing you'll be asking for slippers and dressing gowns and a squad of nursemaids."

The chair squeaked as he shifted his weight. "Nursemaids," he muttered. "I'll nursemaid that jackass when I see him again. Even if he does outrank me."

The finger drumming began again. It stopped short as Captain McKay realized he was keeping time with the humming from behind the partition. He stood up and strode to the doorway and looked out where his sweating sod crews were raising the walls of the second barracks. "Buckner!" he bellowed. He saw the solid, chunky figure of Corporal Clint Buckner turn and start toward him, and he swung back to his table desk.

The side edge of the canvas partition folded back, and the cheerful face of Mrs. McKay appeared around it. "You be nice to that boy. He found me some more flowers this morning."

"Boy?" said Captain McKay. "He's seen thirty years if a day. Spent most of them doing things a boy wouldn't. Or shouldn't. I don't mean picking flowers."

Sweat gleamed on the broad face and dripped from the broad chin and rolled in little streams down the bare peeling chest of Corporal Clint as he came to attention before the table desk. Not even the heat had wilted the jaunty manner that often stirred in Captain McKay brief memories of his own cocksure youth. "Rest," said Captain McKay, and Corporal Clint relaxed all over and began to appreciate the shaded interior of the room.

Captain McKay clasped his hands behind his head with his elbows flung wide. He noted that the canvas hung undisturbed, but there was no humming behind it. He noted too the wary what's-coming-now look on Corporal Clint's face. "Buckner," he said. "How many times have you been busted and had to earn that stripe all over again?"

"Not so often, sir. Only about four times, sir."

"And how many times have you been in line for a sergeantcy and missed it for some damnfoolishness or other?"

Corporal Clint had the tone pegged now. His face exploded in a grin. "Reckon I've lost count on that, sir. But I'll make it yet."

"Maybe," said Captain McKay. "At least I'm giving you a chance. I'm giving you ten days and fifteen dollars and

Cat Nipped

telling you to go find me some cats. Go easy on the money. It's coming out of my own pocket. My guess is there ain't a cat yet in the whole of Kansas Territory. But it was your notion, and now you're stuck with it. You bring me some cats, and the other stripe's yours."

Corporal Clint Buckner woke with the first light of dawn through the open doorway of the dugout. He lay on a thin matting of straw on the dirt floor of this one place that offered any accommodations at all for thirty miles in either direction along the wagon trace outside. He was not alone. His host, a beard-matted trader, was snoring two feet away. A pair of lank and odorous mule skinners lay like logs on the other side of the doorway. And the straw had a moving multitude of its own inhabitants.

Corporal Clint sat up and ruffled bits of straw out of his hair. Four of his ten days and a large part of the fifteen dollars were gone. It was time to start looking for cats in earnest. He had covered considerable territory already and made casual inquiries, but there had been no pressure in the search. Two whole days he had wasted in the one settlement within a hundred miles of the post. Well, not exactly wasted. The settlement boasted no cat, but it did boast a pert waitress at the false-fronted building called a hotel. She had slapped him the first time he kissed her. She had forgotten to slap the second time. He might have been there yet if her husband had not come home with a wagonload of potatoes and turnips and a positive itch to lambast anyone interested in her. Corporal Clint had no aversion to fighting, any place and any time, but it was against his principles to fight husbands.

Outside by the well he stripped himself bare and sloshed himself thoroughly with several buckets of water. While his skin dried in the early-morning air he conducted a careful search through his clothes to eliminate any visitors from the straw. "Wouldn't want to kidnap any of these critters," he said. "Now if they were only cats. . . ."

Dressed again, he caught his horse in the small-pole corral by the dugout and saddled and started off. He was traveling light in boots and pants and shirt and hat. His saddleroll consisted of a blanket, a razor, and an empty grain bag with a few holes punched near the top. He had a vague notion of carrying any cats he might collect in the bag. His armament consisted of a standard cavalry pistol in a snap-shut holster on his left hip and the cherished carbine in a saddle scabbard. He had a long day's route mapped in his mind to cover the far-scattered squatters' roosts and ranch stations within a wide radius.

The welcome slight coolness of evening found Corporal Clint Buckner atop a long rolling ridge that gave him a view of several hundred square miles of catless Kansas. He was a tired and downcast man. As usual the more tired and downcast he was, the more determined he became. "Legwork won't do it," he said. "Like hunting a needle in a hell of a big haystack without even knowing a needle's there. This calls for heavy thinking."

He dismounted and let the horse graze while he studied the problem. There were several villages of friendly Indians within reaching distance, but Indians didn't have cats. They likely wouldn't even know what a cat was. Only white settlers who might bring them from back East would ever have cats. At that, only a few would do it. Cats weren't good travelers like dogs. They had to be carried in the wagons and were a nuisance. They wandered off and were left behind or got lost or some bigger animals made meals of them. But settlers offered the only possible chance. New settlers, those fresh out from back East a ways.

In the cool of the dark Corporal Clint picketed his horse. He was ten miles farther south near the deepening road ruts of the main route of the emigrant wagon trains heading farther west to pick up the Santa Fe Trail. He lay quiet, rolled in his blankets, and watched the nearly full moon rise over the left-hand ridge. "Just one of the scratching little brutes," he said, "and I'll make the old man give me that stripe."

Refreshed and jaunty in the morning sun, Corporal Clint rode along beside the wagon ruts. As he rode he hummed a small wordless tune. He had breakfast with an emigrant family, exchanging advice on the best route ahead for his food and edging around at last to the subject in hand. "Cats?" said the man. "Why sure, we had one. Coyote got it two days back."

Corporal Clint rode on, jauntier than before. "On the right track now," he said. He began humming again, and after a while his small tune had words.

> I'm hunting a feline critter
> Some people call a cat.
> To me any day it's a sergeant's pay—
> A new feather in my hat.

Ten hours, seventy miles, three wagon trains, and two

ranch stations later, no longer jaunty, Corporal Clint dismounted by a small stream and unsaddled before he led the horse to the water. There were several hours of daylight left, but the horse was done for the day. He could have pushed it farther, but he had the true cavalryman's respect for his mount. He fastened the picket rope and sat on a slight rise near the stream and chewed on the sandwiches he had collected at his last stop. "There ain't a cat between here and Missouri," he said. "Wonder if a gelded skunk might do."

He finished the sandwiches and plucked a blade of grass and chewed it long and thoughtfully. Far to the east along the rutted trail a small dust cloud rose and grew and drifted in the freshening breeze. It came closer, always renewed, and beneath it and moving in it were men on horseback and oxteams straining into yokes to pull a motley collection of wagons. They came closer and swung past in an arc to line up and stop along the bank of the stream.

Corporal Clint chewed on his grass-blade and watched the wagons swing past. The third wagon was driven by a faded woman in a faded sunbonnet and beside her on the seat sat a brighter, sharper-colored copy with no sunbonnet to cramp a tumbled glory of dark brown hair. Corporal Clint forgot to chew and stared at this second woman. "Man alive," he said, "that's a mighty attractive sight." He leaned forward and stared some more. "Yes, sir," he said. "Without any argufying or equivocating whatsomever, that's the most attractive sight I ever sighted." The woman had seen him on his knoll and had turned to look at him as the wagon swung past. Curled in her lap was a cat.

* * *

126

Cat Nipped

Corporal Clint Buckner was helpful to have around. He helped the man unyoke the third wagon and water the oxen and picket them along with the man's horse by some good grass. He was expert at finding buffalo chips for the fire in places overlooked by previous overnight campers. And he was a contagious and shrewd talker. By the time cooking smells were drifting around, he had adequate information in hand. The man and the faded woman, his wife, were headed for California. The other woman was the wife's sister. Her name was Ellen. The cat belonged to her, and it was a damn nuisance too. The man didn't think much of this sister business. She was too independent and she thought she knew all there was to know and she made too much fuss over animals and she was another mouth to feed, but his wife had nagged him into letting her come along.

Corporal Clint squatted on his heels and sniffed the cooking smells. "Why sure, ma'am," he said to the faded woman, "I've only had four meals so far today so of course I'll join you. Ain't often I get me real woman's cooking."

Corporal Clint squatted on his heels by the stream bank and watched the sister rinsing off the dishes. "Miss Ellen," he said, "that cat must be a trouble to you on a jaunt like this. If you're so minded, I'd do you the favor of taking it off your hands. Give it a nice home at my quarters."

Corporal Clint leaned against a wagon wheel and looked down at Miss Ellen on a stool plying a needle with knowing skill. "Tell you what," he said, "I always was seven kinds a fool. I'll give you a dollar for that cat."

Corporal Clint stood straight and solid and indignant and glared at Miss Ellen shaking out blankets before making up beds under the wagon. He calculated what remained in his pocket. "Miss Ellen," he said, "you're the obstinatest female I ever met. That cat's just a scrawny, mangy, piebald sort of thing. But I'll give you four dollars and thirty-seven cents for it."

Miss Ellen faced him, not as solid but just as indignant. "Mr. Soldier. That's a good healthy cat, and you're a mangy sort of thing to say it isn't. I've told you and told you it's not for sale. It's my cat. It stays with me. It goes where I go. Now you go do some soldiering and stop bothering me."

Corporal Clint lay sleepless in his blanket on his knoll and watched the almost full moon climb the sky. "Could sneak down there now they're asleep," he said. "Nab the critter, leave the money, make some tracks." The moon climbed higher. "No," he said. "Can't do that to a woman." He lay on one side for a while and then on the other, and the ground seemed uncommonly hard. "If I'm going to get places in this damned Army," he said, "I got to get started soon. I need that stripe." The moon arched overhead and started its downward sweep, and still his eyes remained open. "So it goes where she goes," he said. "Got to keep that in mind." He squirmed on the ground and sat up and hunted under the blanket and removed a small stone and lay quiet again. "Awful lot to ask of a man," he said, "just to get hold of a cat." The moon dropped toward the horizon, and he began figuring the time he had left. Four days. One would be needed for the return to the post. Three days. Nights too. It would work out about right. In that time, the way the train was headed, it would be close to a meeting with the regular mail wagon bound for the post.

128

Cat Nipped

"Shucks," he said. "She's unattached and she's a woman. That's plenty of time. Even got me a full moon coming on schedule."

In the early light of morning Miss Ellen held fast to the handle of a bucket of water as Corporal Clint Buckner tried to take it from her. "I'm quite capable of carrying this myself. And if you say one word about my cat, I'll dump this water right over your grinning head."

"Cat?" said Corporal Clint. "Oh, you mean that pet of yours. Shucks, ma'am, I was only pretending to be interested in that cat trying to please you, you're so fond of it. Took one look at you coming along in that wagon and haven't been able to think of a thing else ever since but trying to please you."

Corporal Clint Buckner was very helpful to have around. He was on hand wherever help was needed along the wagon line, particularly in the neighborhood of the third wagon. Neither heat nor dust dimmed his cheerfulness. He knew the best camping places. He knew every kink in the trail and a cutoff that saved ten miles. He rode away across the prairie and out of sight, and Miss Ellen watched him go with a speculative look in her eyes. He rode back with the carcass of an antelope over the withers of his horse, and Miss Ellen watched him come back with a half smile on her lips and found her hands fussing with her hair. Corporal Clint knew his way around in many ways. Walking with her in the moonlight, he wasted no time talking about cats.

In the relative cool of approaching evening, Corporal

Clint stood by the unyoked wagon and watched Miss Ellen and her sister making antelope stew. He felt a familiar warning prickling on his skin and looked down the arc of bedded wagons and saw two men coming toward him, the two men, youngish and healthy and hefty in the shoulders, who herded the milk cows and spare oxen that tagged the train. He had the notion from the way they had looked at him now and again that their opinion of him was not flattering. They were looking at him now, and their forward tread was full of purpose.

"Soldier," said the first one, "me and Bert been talking about you. We been watching you. We don't like it. We decided a couple weeks back Miss Ellen was going to have one of us and she'd have to pick which when we get where we're going. We decided now it's time you—"

"Oh-h-h-h," said Miss Ellen. "I guess I have something to say about that."

No one paid any attention to her, not even Corporal Clint. He was inspecting the two men, and his eyes were beginning to brighten.

"That's right," said Bert. "We just don't like it. Three days you been hanging around Miss Ellen. Last night was my night and night before was Jeb's, but when we come looking she wasn't around. She was gallivanting off with you somewheres. We decided you better start traveling."

"Well, well," said Corporal Clint. "Ain't it too bad I don't feel any traveling urge."

"We decided mebbe you wouldn't," said Bert. "We decided we'd just have to give it to you."

They stepped forward. Corporal Clint stepped to meet them. With a grin on his face and a gleam of joy in his

130

eyes, Corporal Clint moved into battle. He bent low and drove his broad head like a cannonball into Bert's middle and straightened and swung to work on Jeb with experienced fists. Bert rolled on the ground and groaned.

"Oh-h-h-h," said Miss Ellen, and ran to bend over Bert, "you poor man. Did he break your ribs?"

Corporal Clint heard. He saw. His blows began to go wild. They missed Jeb entirely or when they hit they no longer carried a powerful jolt. He winced when Jeb struck him and began to retreat. Jeb rushed at him, hot with encouragement, and Bert struggled to his feet and gulped in air and plunged to join Jeb. Together they battered Corporal Clint. The air hummed with sweeping fists. Corporal Clint went down. He groaned. He staggered to his feet. He went down again. His groan was a plaintive and appealing sound. His body twitched and was still.

"Oh-h-h-h-h," said Miss Ellen. She stood beside his prone body and smacked at Bert and Jeb with her words. "You cowards! Two of you beating him!"

Bert and Jeb stepped backward. "Why, Miss Ellen," said Jeb. "We just decided—"

"Who cares what you decided?" said Miss Ellen. "I hate the sight of both of you. You get away from here and back with those cows, which is just about all you're fit to associate with." As Bert and Jeb retired in confusion she ran to the wagon and dipped a cloth in the water bucket and ran back to raise Corporal Clint's limp head with one hand and wipe off his bruised dusty face with the other. Corporal Clint opened his eyes. "You have such nice hands," he said, and groaned again, a small satisfied groan, and closed his eyes.

Half an hour later, limping painfully, Corporal Clint edged around the wagon. Out of sight behind it, he strode off toward the rear of the line of wagons. The limp disappeared, and he strode with a purposeful stride. He found Bert and Jeb squatted by a fire downing third cups of coffee in sullen discouragement. "Stand up, boys," he said. "We'll take up now where we left off." With the same grin on his bruised face and gleam of joy in his half-closed eyes, Corporal Clint moved into battle. Seven minutes later he looked down upon Bert and Jeb reclining dazed and much more discouraged on the ground. "Take a bit of advice," he said. "Don't go deciding to interfere with the Army again." He strode back the way he had come behind the line of wagons, and as he went the limp began once more and became more pronounced with each step, and as he limped he caroled his small tune to himself with new words.

> I found me a feline critter—
> A lady's personal pet.
> Goes where she goes but I'm one knows
> It won't be hard to get.

Walking with Miss Ellen in the moonlight, he endured his limp with gallant fortitude. It forced him to lean some on her for support and to put an arm over her shoulders.

The light mail wagon rolled steadily over the prairie. Fifty yards ahead the escort, two privates and a lance corporal, trotted steadily forward and with them, happy at freedom from constant sitting on a board seat, trotted the

132

regular driver astride Corporal Clint Buckner's horse. In the wagon, jaunty and cheerful with the reins in his hands, sat Corporal Clint and behind him, between the mail bag and a box, was a woman's trunk and beside him sat Miss Ellen and curled in her lap was the cat.

The miles slipped away under the wheels. "Clint," said Miss Ellen, "my head's been in such a whirl I didn't think before. Is there a preacher at the post?"

"Preacher?" said Corporal Clint. "Whatever for?"

"Why, to marry us, silly."

"Shucks," said Corporal Clint. "We don't need a preacher. The old man, that's the captain, he's got authority to do the job right and even better."

"A military ceremony!" said Miss Ellen. "That'll be fun. Will they cross swords for us?"

"Sabers," said Corporal Clint. "I ain't a commissioned officer so it won't be too fancy."

More miles slipped away. "Clint," said Miss Ellen, "you're a sergeant, aren't you? You said so. But there's only one stripe on your sleeve."

"Well, I am," said Corporal Clint, not quite as jaunty as before. "In a manner of speaking I am. I mean I will be when I get back there."

"Oh," said Miss Ellen. "You're being promoted you mean. I knew you'd be the kind of man who gets promotions. What did you do to get this one?"

"Shucks," said Corporal Clint, "nothing much. Just a little special duty." He began to notice that it was a hot and dusty day.

They stopped for a midday meal and to rest the horses. Corporal Clint strutted some, giving orders because he was the ranking man present, but his voice lacked its usual confident clip. He chewed in a strange silence, very thoughtful. The cat wandered about forty feet away, intent on its own individual business. Corporal Clint leaped to his feet and raced to grab it and bring it back. He smiled weakly at Miss Ellen. "Dangerous country," he said. "Coyotes and things around."

They drove forward again, and Corporal Clint was restless on the wagon seat. Miss Ellen did not notice. She had missed most of her sleep the night before, and the slight swaying of the wagon as it rolled easily along the trace among the grass tufts made her drowsy. She pulled his right arm about her and snuggled close and rested her head, half dozing, on his shoulder. Corporal Clint could feel her hair blowing softly against his cheek in the breeze of their movement and his shirt suddenly felt too small around his chest and this was very nice hair brushing his check and he knew he should be pleased, but he was too bothered by troublesome thoughts to appreciate the pleasure.

The miles dropped away beneath the hooves and the wheels, and they came to a shallow stream and splashed into it. The front wheel on Corporal Clint's side hit a stone and rose up on it tilting the wagon. Miss Ellen slid on the seat squealing and clutching at him, and the cat tumbled out of her lap into the water. Corporal Clint yanked on the reins and dropped them and scrambled past Miss Ellen to follow the cat. He landed on all fours in the eight inches of water, scrabbled about in it, and rose dripping with the cat in his arms.

"Good grief!" said Miss Ellen. "You didn't even bother about me but just that cat."

Cat Nipped

"Might have been a pool over on this side," said Corporal Clint, trying to smile at her and failing. "Might have been real deep water."

"Silly," said Miss Ellen. "Maybe cats don't like water, but they can swim all right if they have to. Well, I suppose it's nice you worrying so about that cat just because I like it so. I hope you don't catch the sniffles now."

"It ain't sniffles I'm worried about catching," said Corporal Clint.

The afternoon sun was low on the left as the mail wagon topped the last swell of the prairie that gave a clear view of the beginnings of Fort McKay in the distance. "That's it," said Corporal Clint Buckner with little of a prospective bridegroom's joy in his voice. His eyes brightened. "Maybe I'd better get on my horse and hurry on in ahead to sort of prepare the way some."

"And leave me?" said Miss Ellen. "I think we should drive in together. I want to see how surprised everyone is, too. And don't worry what I'll think about how you behave. I know you have to salute and stand at attention and things like that."

The escort dropped respectfully to the rear to tail the wagon in. Corporal Clint's face grew pale as he saw they had been sighted coming and the entire personnel of the post was assembling for a good view. It grew paler as he saw that Captain McKay, contrary to custom at this hour, was not in his quarters but was standing outside with Mrs. McKay beside him. Corporal Clint sighed. Then he straightened on the seat and snapped back his shoulders and cocked his head at a jaunty angle. He urged the team into a faster trot. He pulled up close to Captain

McKay with a flourish and jumped to the ground. His salute was a gesture of swift and precise perfection. "Reporting for duty, sir. Right on the tenth day, sir. Brought a young lady with me, sir, who has done me the honor of consenting to become my wife, sir. With your permission, of course, sir. I'm asking for same now, sir. And to perform the ceremony yourself, sir. As soon as—"

"But—" said Captain McKay. "But—but—"

"Awfully sudden, sir," said Corporal Clint. "But it had to be that way. Begging your pardon, sir, but I can report later. Bring her around for official introduction later too, sir. Really ought to be fixing her some quarters right away, sir. It's been a long drive. And dusty. She'll want to rest first, sir, and clean up some before a formal meeting. If you'll just let me have a tent, sir, I can fix—"

"But—" said Captain McKay. "But—but I sent you out to get some cats."

"Oh-h-h-h-h-h," said Miss Ellen.

"I told you I'd report later, sir." Corporal Clint took another breath. "Explain everything then, sir. I've done my duty. Done the best I could, sir. Things kind of happened and turned out this way. All for the best all around, sir. If you'll just let me have a tent—"

"Shut up!" bellowed Captain McKay. "I don't know what particular breed of devilment you've pulled this time, but I know it's all of a piece with past behavior. Send you out with orders to find some cats, and you come back bringing another woman to this Godforsaken place that ain't fit—"

"But she's got a cat, sir," said Corporal Clint.

"Oh-h-h-h," said Miss Ellen. "So that's why you were

136

so interested in my cat! And jumping after it all the time without caring what happened to me! Talking about marrying just to trick me into coming here so maybe you could steal it!"

"I did not," said Corporal Clint. "That's not right. That's—"

"I hate you," said Miss Ellen. "I just plain utterly despise you. Taking me away from the only folks I had and making it all sound so nice when it isn't at all. I wouldn't marry you now even if—well, I just wouldn't—I wouldn't—" Suddenly Miss Ellen was crying and she was ashamed to be crying in front of a group of startled and embarrassed men and she put her head down in her arms and the cat slipped out of her lap and retreated over the seat into the rear of the wagon and she was sitting there with her shoulders shaking.

"Humph!" snorted Mrs. McKay. "A fine mess you men've made now. But then you always do. Where a woman's concerned anyway. Yelling at each other. Blathering about cats. A nice lovely girl like that too." She marched to the wagon and cooed soft reassurances at Miss Ellen and helped her down from the seat. In a silence made ominous by the expression on Captain McKay's face she led Miss Ellen into the captain's quarters. They disappeared from sight.

"Buckner," said Captain McKay. His tone was mild and deadly. "You have committed so damn many offenses under the military code from the moment you started yapping at me before I gave you permission to speak that I won't even try to list them now. God only knows what devilish things you've been doing while you were gone, but I intend to find out. You're under arrest. Go to your quarters and stay there till I decide what to do with you. While you're there improve your time taking that stripe off your sleeve."

Captain McKay wiped his forehead and turned to go inside and face Mrs. McKay and Miss Ellen. Surrounded by his fellows and a babble of jeering and commiserating and even envious voices, Corporal Clint moved toward the double row of tents. The mail escort rode forward, and one of them dismounted and climbed to the wagon seat to drive it over by the stable. "Wait a moment," said Lieutenant Henley, pushing out from the shade of one of the sod-walled buildings. He leaned over the backboard of the wagon and reached inside and lifted out the cat.

Private Clint Buckner sat on a three-legged stool in the end tent of the front row facing the stretch of level ground that would someday be the parade ground and stared out into the morning sun. Somehow it was hotter under the canvas than it would have been outside under the open sun with a sod crew. The heat was personal, oppressive, made so by the silence, the solitude of that particular corner of the post, and his complete ignorance of what was happening in Captain McKay's quarters and adjacent areas.

He twisted on his stool to get a better view. Across the way there was a flurry of unusual activity. Sergeant Peattie appeared with a squad of fast-stepping privates carrying various things, and walking beside him, pert and chipper with her dark brown hair a tumbled glory about her head, was Miss Ellen. Private Clint could see that Sergeant

Cat Nipped

Peattie was unusually neat and natty and was strutting to good effect and barking orders with obvious relish. The squad stopped and began to erect a tent almost exactly opposite the one in which Private Clint sat in his solitude and close to the bend in the lazy almost dried-up little river that ran alongside the post. The tent went up quickly and was pegged tight. Into it went a cot, a chair, a washstand made of a box set on end with a cloth covering the open side, and Miss Ellen's trunk.

The squad was gone. Even Sergeant Peattie, who had lingered long, was gone. The flaps of the newly erected tent were closed. "Can't any more than shoot me," said Private Clint. He crawled under the rear canvas of his tent and set off on a wide circuit, bent low and crawling at times, taking advantage of all possible cover. He came up behind Miss Ellen's tent. He lifted its rear canvas and poked his head under. "Good morning, ma'am."

Miss Ellen was busy at her trunk. She jumped around, startled. She stared at the broad face peering up turtle-wise. "Oh, it's you," she said.

"It's me all right," said Private Clint. He crawled the rest of the way under and perched himself on the chair. "I'm mighty peeved too. If you'd only had sense enough to keep your yap shut—"

"Mr. Buckner," said Miss Ellen, "all I have to do is yell, and you'll be—"

"Go ahead and yell," said Private Clint. "Another charge or two won't mean much to me now. I want to know what the hell—and I won't ask pardon for that either—is going on over here."

"Why, Mr. Buckner," said Miss Ellen, very sweetly. "I

don't figure you have any right to know, but I'll tell you. Everybody's being so nice to me. That Lieutenant Henley's taking good care of my cat, and he says it's just a marvelous mouser. And this tent is all my own and I'm to have a better place soon as more buildings are up and it'll be fixed real nice and I'm to be the officers' laundress and have my meals with the McKays and get right good pay too."

Private Clint groaned. He tried to make his voice plaintive. "But what about me?"

"You?" said Miss Ellen. "I don't know as that's any concern of mine. I have myself to worry about, seeing as you got me in such a fix. I think I'm doing right well." Miss Ellen reached up and fluffed her hair. "Maybe you've not noticed, being a man, but that Sergeant Peattie is a fine-looking man himself."

"Peattie," moaned Private Clint. "You watch out for him. I've been on leaves with him, and I'm telling you—"

"He's told me plenty about you," said Miss Ellen. "Now I remember what he's told me I think it's time you crawled out of here and stayed away."

"Shucks," said Private Clint. "Peattie always did stretch things too far. How about you remembering those nights when the moon—"

"I will not!" Miss Ellen stamped one foot and glared at him. "You get out of here now, or I really will yell!"

"Damn woman," muttered Private Clint, as he crawled under the canvas. "Always being so damn womanish." The last he saw before he let the canvas drop and departed on his return circuit was Miss Ellen standing straight and glaring at him and prettier than he'd remembered her all through the previous night. What he did not see and what Mrs. McKay did see five minutes later, as she pushed through the tent flaps with her arms laden with blankets and a mirror, was Miss Ellen slumped on the chair and crying.

Captain McKay stomped into his office hot and dusty from his afternoon jaunt to inspect his work crews at their labors. For an instant he thought he had been hearing voices from behind the canvas partition as he entered, but now there was no sound. He listened. A soft melodic humming began and he relaxed. His wife indulged in that silly humming only when she was alone. He sat behind his table desk and wiped dust from his face. The canvas partition folded back at the front edge, and Mrs. McKay's face appeared around it followed by the rest of her.

"Mac," she said, "you've left that Buckner boy sweating in that tent and wondering what you're going to do all last night and most of today. Don't you think it's time you had him over here to speak up for himself?"

"Speak up?" said Captain McKay. "He spoke up so damn much yesterday I've a mind to let him squat over there the rest of the summer. If we were back anywhere near civilization and he behaved like that and I didn't have his hide, there's plenty other officers'd think I was losing my grip."

Mrs. McKay simply looked at her husband and smiled a small smile. "Oh, I know," he said. "We're way out here the end of nowhere, and I'm top dog and I can do about anything I damn well please. So I'm just letting him sit there awhile meditating on his sins. It'll do him good."

"Mac," said Mrs. McKay, "he's the only one out here, yourself included, ever thought to find me flowers. He's talked a girl you've been making sheep's eyes at yourself into coming here to marry him, and now he's talked himself under arrest and into having her think mighty small of him. Sometimes I think you're not the same man I married twenty-too-many years ago." The canvas partition folded back again, and Mrs. McKay disappeared behind it.

Captain McKay sat still, drumming his fingers and remembering many things. He rose and went to the doorway and out a short distance. "Buckner!" he bellowed across the level space and remembered bellowing that same name in that same voice when he and his command were pinned down in small scattered groups in a dry stream bed by many times their own number of hostile Indians and he needed a man who might be just reckless enough and tough enough to get through with a message for reinforcements. The thought flashed through his mind that likely he'd be bellowing that same name again when the settlers his post and others were supposed to protect began coming in real numbers to populate the Territory and the Indians got worried again about losing their lands and made trouble. He returned and sat again behind his table desk and made himself look stern and official.

Private Clint Buckner stood before him with that what's-coming-now look on his face.

"Buckner," said Captain McKay, "how much of my fifteen dollars have you got left?"

"Four dollars and thirty-seven cents, sir."

Captain McKay thumped a fist on the table. "Better'n ten dollars gone, and you didn't spend a nickel on cats.

Cat Nipped

I've heard the girl's story. By rights I ought to skin you alive and hang your hide out to dry. Maybe I will yet. First I want you to tell me how you got yourself in such a fool fix."

"Well, sir," said Private Clint, "you wanted cats. I couldn't find cats. Well, sir, I found one and it was attached to that Miss Ellen woman and she wouldn't sell it. I figured the only way to get it here was get her here. I figured the only way to get her here was to marry her. You're a man, sir. You know how it is. It seemed a kind of good idea at the time."

"Damned if I do know how it is," said Captain McKay. "It's never crossed my mind to marry a woman to get a cat."

"That's only how it started, sir. More I saw of her the more I figured it was a good idea all by itself. She's a mighty attractive woman, sir."

"In a sort of way," said Captain McKay, conscious of Mrs. McKay behind the partition. "But she says it's plain you've been interested mostly in that cat all the time. Says you paid more attention to it coming here than to her. Says you were willing to about knock her out of the wagon to save that cat from a little water."

"That's all backwards," said Private Clint. "That cat gives me a pain just thinking of it. You see, sir, when we headed here I got to thinking. I got to thinking what a real chunk of woman she is. Nerve enough to leave that wagon train and the only folks she knew and go to a place she didn't know a thing about and take a chance on a cross-branded Army mule like me. That's my kind of woman, sir. I got to thinking the only way I'd ever keep up with her and take care of her the way I ought was being a sergeant. That's the cat. I had to keep it safe. You promised me if I—"

"So-o-o-o," said Captain McKay. "A hell of a soldier you are. Conducted your campaign without thinking through to the finish. Forgot till too late how your fine talk would sound to her when she found out about the cat. Walked right into what I'd call a verbal ambush. Now you've lost out all around. Lost the girl. Lost the sergeantcy. I distinctly told you cats. Plural. You brought just one."

The partition folded back and around it came Mrs. McKay. Behind her and moving up beside her came Miss Ellen. Miss Ellen's head was held high, and her eyes were bright. "Captain McKay," she said, "that cat is cats." Miss Ellen blushed very prettily and looked at Private Clint and looked away and blushed even more prettily. "That cat had an—well, an—affair with another cat back in Springfield when we came through. It won't be long now. She always has four or five at a time."

Captain McKay looked at Miss Ellen blushing so prettily. He looked at Private Clint Buckner, who was looking at Miss Ellen with his head at a jaunty angle and a grin on his broad face. He looked at Mrs. McKay, who was looking at him with that expectant expression that meant he had better do something and it had better be the right thing. He cleared his throat. "Sergeant Buckner, you will report back here directly after mess in the neatest uniform you can beg, borrow, or steal around this post. You may regard the fifteen dollars as a wedding present. The ceremony will be at seven o'clock."

144

Total Loss

SYLVIA TOWNSEND WARNER

When Charlotte woke, it was raining. Rain hid the view
of the downs and blurred the neat row of trees and the
neat row of houses opposite which the trees had been
planted to screen. This was the third wet morning since
her birthday a week ago. There would be rain all through
the holidays, just like last year. On her birthday, Charlotte was ten. "Now you are in double figures," said Professor Bayer. "And you will stay in them till you are a
hundred years old. Think of that, my Lottchen."

"Yes, think of that," said Mother.

145

Charlotte could see that Mother did not really wish to think of it. She was being polite, because Professor Bayer was a very important person at the Research Station, so it was a real honor that he should like Father and come to the house to borrow *The New Statesman*.

Charlotte's cat Moodie was awake already. He lay on the chair in the corner, on top of her clothes, and was staring at her with a thirsty expression. She jumped out of bed, went to the kitchen, breaking into its early-morning tidiness and seclusion, and came back with a saucer of milk. "Look, Moodie! Nice milk." He would not drink, though he still had that thirsty expression. "You silly old Moodles, you don't know what you want," she said, kneeling before the chair with the saucer in her hand. Moodie had come as a wedding present to Mother. His birthday was unknown, but he was certainly two years older than Charlotte. Ever since she could remember, there had been Moodie, and Moodie had been hers—to be slept on, talked to, hauled about, wheeled in a doll's perambulator, read aloud to, confided in, wept on, trodden on, loved, and taken for granted. He stared at her, ignoring the milk, and forgetting the milk she stared back, fascinated as ever by the way the fur grew on his nose, the mysterious smooth conflict between two currents of growth. At last she put down the saucer, seized him in her arms, and got back into bed. "We understand each other, don't we?" she said, curling his tail round his flank. "Don't we, Moodie?" He trod with his front paws, purring under his breath, and relaxed, his head on her breast. But at the smell of his bad teeth she turned her face away, pretending it was to look out the window. "It's raining, Moodie. It's going to be another horrible wet day. You mustn't be a silly cat, sitting in the garden and getting wet through, like you did on Tuesday." He was still purring when she fell asleep, though when her mother came to wake her he had gone. Sure enough, when she looked for him after breakfast, he was sitting hunched and motionless on the lawn, his gray fur silvered with moisture and fluffed out like a coat of eiderdown. She picked him up, and the bloom vanished; the eiderdown coat, suddenly dark and lank, clung to his bony haunches. "Mother, I'm going to put Moodie in the airing cupboard."

"Yes, do, my pet. That's the best plan! But hurry, because Mr. and Mrs. Flaxman will be here to fetch you at any moment. They've just rung up. They want you to spend the day with them."

"And see the horses?"

The cat in the child's arms broke into a purr, as though her thrill of pleasure communicated itself to him. Though of course it was really the warmth of the kitchen, thought Charlotte's mother, Meg Atwood.

"Yes, the horses. And the bantams. And the lovely old toy theater that belonged to Mrs. Flaxman's grandmother. You'll love it. It's an absolutely storybook house."

"Shall I wear my new mac?"

"Yes. But hurry, Charlotte. Put Moodie in the airing cupboard, and wash your hands. I'll be up in a moment to brush your hair."

She had made one false step. The Flaxmans lived twenty miles away, and if they had just rung up they could not be arriving immediately. Luckily Charlotte, though brought up to use her reason, was not a very deductive child; the discrepancy between the prompt arriving of the Flaxmans and the long drive back to Hood House was not likely to catch her attention. But perhaps a private word to Adela Flaxman—just to be on the safe side.

"Mother! Mother!"

At the threatening woe of the cry, Meg left everything and ran.

"Mother! There's a button off."

The Flaxmans arrived, both talking at once, and saying what a horrible day it was, and "Oh, the wretched farmers, who would be a farmer?" in loud, gay voices. Mrs. Flaxman was Mother's particular friend, but today Mother didn't seem to like her so much and was laughing obligingly, just as she did with Professor Bayer. As Charlotte stood on the outskirts of this conversation she began to feel less sure of a happy successful day out. She would be treated like a child and probably given milk instead of tea. Moodie hadn't drunk that milk. "Mother! Don't forget to feed Moodie."

"Charlotte! As if I would—"

At the same moment, Mr. Flaxman said, "Come on, Charlotte! Come on, Adela! The car will catch cold if you don't hurry," and swept them out of the house.

Meg went slowly upstairs, noticing that the sound of the rain was more insistent in the upper story of the house. The airing cupboard was in the bathroom. She glanced in quickly and closed the door. She gave the room a rapid tidy, went down, and turned on the wireless.

Meg believed in method. Every morning of the week had its program; and this was Thursday, when she defrosted the refrigerator, polished the silver, and turned out

148

her bedroom—a full morning's work. But today she did none of it, wandering about with a desultory, fidgeting tidiness, taking things up and putting them down again, straightening books on their shelves, nipping dead leaves off the houseplants, while the wireless went on with the Daily Service. There was bound to be a *mauvais quart d'heure*. In fact, everything was well in hand; Charlotte was safely disposed of with the Flaxmans, Moodie was asleep in the airing cupboard, and the vet had promised to arrive before midday. It would be quite painless and over in a few minutes. But it was, for all that, a *mauvais quart d'heure*. There are some women, Meg was one of them, in whom conscience is so strongly developed that it leaves little room for anything else. Love is scarcely felt before duty rushes to encase it, anger is impossible because one must always be calm and see both sides, pity evaporates in expedients, even grief is felt as a sort of bruised sense of injury, a resentment that one should have grief forced upon one when one has always acted for the best. Meg's conscience told her that she was acting for the best: Moodie would be spared inevitable suffering, Charlotte protected from a possibly quite serious trauma, Alan undisturbed in his work. Her own distress—and she was fond of poor old Moodie, no other cat could quite replace him because of his associations—was a small price to pay for all these satisfactory arrangements, and she was ready to pay it, sacrificing her own feelings as duty bid and as common sense also bid. Besides, it would soon be over. The trouble about an active, strongly developed conscience is that it requires to be constantly fed with good works, a routine shoveling of meritorious activities. And when you have done everything for the best and are waiting about for the vet to come and kill your old cat and can't, therefore, begin to defrost a refrigerator or turn out a bedroom, a good conscience soon leaves off being a support and becomes a liability, demanding to be supported itself.

The bad quarter of an hour stretched into half an hour, into an hour, into an hour and a quarter, while Meg, stiffening at the noise of every approaching car and fancying with every gust of a fitful rising wind that Moodie was demanding with yowls to be let out of the airing cupboard, tried to read but could not, looked for cobwebs but found none, and wondered if for this once she would break her rule of not drinking spirits before lunchtime. She was in the kitchen, devouring lumps of sugar, when the vet arrived. She took him to the bathroom, opened the cupboard door, heard him say, "Well, old man?"

"Is there anything I can do to help?"

"If you could let me have an old towel."

She produced the towel and went to her bedroom, where she opened the window and looked out on the rain and the tossing trees and remembered that everyone must die. At last she heard the basin tap turned on, the vet washing his hands, the water running away.

"Mrs. Atwood. Have you got a box?"

"A box?"

He stood in the passage, a tall, red-faced young man, the picture of health. "Any sort of carton. To take it away in. A sack would do."

She had not remembered that Moodie would require a coffin. In a flurry of guilt she began to search. There was a brown paper carrier, but it would not do. Moodie could not be borne away swinging from the vet's hand. There was the carton the groceries had come in, but it was too small and had Pan Yan Pickles printed on it. At last she found a plain oblong carton, kept because it was solid and serviceable. Deciding on it, she glanced inside and realized that it would not do like that. Moodie could not be put straight into an empty box; there must be some sort of lining, of padding. She tore old newspaper into strips and crumpled the strips to form a mattress, and then, remembering that flowers are given to the dead, she snatched a couple of dahlias from a vase and scattered the petals on top of the newspaper. The vet was standing in the bathroom, averting his eyes from the bidet, the towel neatly folded was balanced on the edge of the basin, and on the bathroom stool was Moodie's unrecognizably shabby, degraded, dead body. Before she realized what she was saying, she had said, "If you'll hold the box, I'd like to put him in."

Yet what else could she say? She owed it to Moodie. She lifted him on her two hands as she had lifted him so often. The unsupported head fell horribly to one side, lolling like the clapper of a bell. She got the body in somehow, and the vet closed the lid of the carton and carried it away. She knew she ought to have thanked him, but she could not speak. She had never seen a dead body before—except on food counters, of course.

She went downstairs and drank a stiffish whisky. Her sense of proportion reasserted itself. One cannot expect to be perfect in any first performance. She had not behaved at all as she had meant to when Charlotte was born. It was a pity about the makeshift box; it was a pity not to have thanked the vet. But the essentials had been secured: Charlotte was safe and happy at Hood House, Alan was happy and busy in his laboratory. Neither of them need ever know what agony is involved in the process of rationally, mercifully, putting an end to an old pet. She would make a quick lunch of bread and cheese, and then be very busy. She heard a distant peal of thunder and welcomed the thought of a good rousing thunderstorm. Something elemental would be releasing. After a few more long, grumbling reverberations the storm moved away, but when she went to defrost the refrigerator she found it darkened and cavernous; the current was off throughout the house. The power lines on Ram Down were always getting struck. She left the refrigerator to natural forces, and as she couldn't use the Hoover either she polished the silver and sat down to do some mending. She was a bad needlewoman; mending kept her mind occupied till a burst of sunlight surprised her by its slant. She had no idea it was so late. Charlotte would be back at any moment.

Just as the current had gone off, leaving the refrigerator darkened and cavernous, the support of a good conscience now withdrew its aid. Charlotte would be back at any moment. Charlotte would have to be told. Time went on. Suppose there had been a car smash? Charlotte mangled and dying at the roadside, and all because she had been got out of the house while the vet was mercifully releasing Moodie? Meg's doing— How could one ever get over such a thing and lead a normal life again?

She was sitting motionless and frantic when Alan came in, switching on the light in the hall.

"Well, Meg, why are you looking so wrought up? Didn't the vet come? Couldn't he do his stuff?"

"Oh, yes, that was all right. But Charlotte's not back."

"When did they say they'd bring her?"

"Adela didn't say exactly. She said, a good long day. But it's long over that. Adela knows how particular I am about bedtime."

"Why not ring up?"

"But I'm sure they must have started by now."

"Well, someone would be about. They've got that cook. What's their number?"

She heard him in the hall, dialing. Then he came back saying the line seemed to be dead. Ten minutes later a car drew up and Charlotte rushed into the house, followed by Mrs. Flaxman.

"Mother, Mother! It's been so marvelous; it's been so thrilling. We were struck by lightning. There was a huge flash, bright blue, and the telephone shot across the room and broke ever so much china, and there was an awful noise of horses screaming their heads off, and Mr. Flaxman tore out to see if the stables had been struck too, and then ran back saying, 'They're all right but our bloody roof's on fire.' And there was burning thatch flying about everywhere, and Mr. Flaxman went up a ladder, and Mrs. Flaxman and I got buckets and buckets of water and handed them up to him. And I was ever so useful, Adela said so, wasn't I, Mrs. Flaxman?"

"I don't know what we'd have done without you, my pet," said Mrs. Flaxman to Charlotte. To Meg, she added, "She got very wet, but we've dried her."

"And then people came rushing up from the village and trod on the bantams."

"No, nothing's insured except the portraits and the horses. Giles won't, on principle. Yes, calamitous, but it could have been worse. No, no, not at all. It's been a pleasure having her."

Adela was gone, leaving the impression of someone from a higher sphere in a hurry to return to its empyrean.

For the present, there was nothing to be done but listen to Charlotte and try not to blame the Flaxmans for having let her get so overexcited. Both parents lit cigarettes and prepared themselves for a spell of entering into their child's world; after all, fifteen minutes earlier, they had been fearing for her life. They smoked and smiled and made appropriate interjections. Suddenly her narrative ran out, and she said, "Where's Moodie?"

For by the time one is ten one knows when one's parents are only pretending to be interested. Back again in a home that had no horses, no bantams, no curly golden armchairs, no portraits of gentlemen in armor and low-necked ladies, was never struck by lightning and gave her no opportunities to be brave and indispensable, Charlotte concentrated on the one faithful satisfaction it afforded and said, "Where's Moodie?"

Mastering a feeling like stage fright, Meg said with composure, "Darling. Moodie's not here."

"Why isn't he? Has he run away? Has anything happened to him?"

"Not exactly that. But he's dead."

"Why? Why is he dead? He was quite well this morning. Why is he dead?"

"You know, darling, poor Moodie hasn't really been feeling well for a long time. He was an old cat. He had an illness."

Charlotte saw Moodie's broad face and his eyes staring at her with that thirsty expression. Moodie was dead.

Total Loss

Mother had explained to her about death, making it seem very ordinary.

"You remember how horrid his breath smelled?"

"Yes. That was his teeth."

"It wasn't only his teeth. It was something inside that was bound to kill him sooner or later. And he would have suffered a great deal. So the vet came and gave him an injection and put him to sleep. It was all over in a minute."

Moodie had gone out and sat in the rain. The child's glance moved to the window and remained fixed on the lawn, so green in the sunset that it was almost golden. It was a French window. Without a word, she opened it and went out.

"Poor Charlotte!" said Alan. "She's taking it very well. I must say, I think you rubbed it in a bit too much. You needn't have said he stank."

Meg repressed the retort that if Alan could have done it so much better he might perfectly well have done so. In silence, they watched Charlotte walking about in the garden. It was a very small garden, newly planted, and the gardens on either side of it were small and newly planted too, only marked off by light railings. To Meg, whose childhood had known a garden with overgrown shrubs, laurel hedges, a disused greenhouse and a toad, it seemed an inadequate place to grieve in, but from the eighteenth century onward people have turned for comfort to the bosom of nature, and Charlotte was doing so now, among the standard roses and the begonias. She walked up and down, round and round, pausing, walking on again. "Going around his old haunts," said Alan. Moodie, as Meg knew, shared her opinion of the garden; he used it to scratch in, but for any serious haunting went to Mopson's

Garage where he and the neighborhood cats clubbed among the derelict cars. A sense of loss pierced her; knowing Moodie's ways had been a kind of illicit Bohemianism in her exemplary, rather lonely life. But it was Charlotte's loss she must think of—and Charlotte's supper, which was long overdue.

"I wish she'd come in, but we mustn't hurry her."

Alan said, "She's coming now."

Charlotte was walking toward the house, walking with a firm tread. Her face was still pale with shock, but her expression was composed, resolved, even excited. I must give her a sedative, thought Meg. Charlotte entered, saying, "I've chosen the place for his grave."

After the bungled explanations that one couldn't, that the lawn would never be the same again, that it wasn't their garden, that the lease expressly forbade burying animals had broken down under the child's cross-examination into an admission that there was no body to bury, that the vet had taken it away, that it could not be got back, that it had been disposed of, that in all probability it had been burned to ashes as her parents' bodies would in due course be burned; after Charlotte, declaring she would never forgive them, never, that they were liars and murderers, that she hated them and hoped they would soon be burned to ashes themselves, had somehow been got to bed, they sat down, exhausted, not looking at each other.

"That damned cat!"

As though Alan's words had unloosed it, a wailing cry came from overhead. "O Moodie, Moodie, Moodie! O Moodie, Moodie, Moodie!"

Implacable as the iteration of waves breaking on a beach,

the wailing cries rang through the house. Twice Meg started to her feet, was told not to be weak-minded, and sat down again. Alan ought to be fed. Something ought to be done. The mere thought of food made her feel sick. Alan was filling his pipe. Staring in front of her, lost in a final imbecility of patience, she found she was looking at the two dahlia stalks whose petals she had torn away.

"O Moodie, Moodie, Moodie!"

The thought of something to be done emerged. "We must put off that new kitten," she said.

"Why?"

Completing her husband's exasperation, Meg buried her face in her hands and began to cry. "O Moodie," she lamented. "Oh, my kind cat!"

The Ninth Life

MAZO DE LA ROCHE

"Harriet! Harriet! Harriet!" Her name echoed through the pipe woods. It echoed across the water to the next island, was flung back from its precipitous shore in a mournful echo. Still she did not come.

The launch stood waiting at the wharf, laden with the luggage attendant on the breaking up of the holiday season. Summer was past, October almost gone, wild geese were mirrored in the lake in their flight southward. Now, for eight months, the Indians and the wild deer would have the islands to themselves.

The Boyds were the last of the summer people to go.

The Ninth Life

They enjoyed the month of freedom at the end of the season, when tourists were gone. They were country people themselves, bred in the district. When they were not living on their island they lived in a small town at the foot of the lake, thirty miles away. The year was marked for them by their migration to the island in the middle of June and their return to winter habitation in October.

They were well-to-do. They owned their launch, which now stood waiting at the wharf, with the Indian, John Nanabush, at the wheel. He stood, dark and imperturbable, while Mrs. Boyd, her daughters, and her cook raised their voices for Harriet. Mr. Boyd prowled about at the back of the cottage, peering into the workshop, the icehouse, behind the woodpile, where freshly cut birch logs lay waiting for next year's fires. Now and again he gave a stentorian shout for Harriet.

They had delayed their departure for hours because of her. Now they must go without her. Mrs. Boyd came to the wide veranda, where the canoe lay covered by canvas. She lifted the edge of the canvas and peered under it.

"Why, Mother, what a place to look!" said her husband. "The cat wouldn't be in there."

"I know," said Mrs. Boyd. "But I just feel so desperate!"

"Well, we've got to go without her."

"And it's getting so cold!"

On the wharf the girls wailed, "Oh, Father, we can't leave Harriet on the island!"

"Find her, Pat! Find Harriet!" said Mr. Boyd to the Irish terrier.

Pat leaped from the launch, where he was investigating the hamper of eatables, and raced up the rocky shore. In his own fashion he shouted for the cat. A chipmunk darted

159

from the trunk of a jack pine, sped across a large, flat rock, ran halfway up a flaming red maple, and paused, upside down, to stare at the group on the wharf.

John Nanabush raised his soft, thick, Indian voice. "You folks go along home. I'll find Harriet. I'll keep her for you."

"That's a good idea," said Mr. Boyd.

"Harriet would never stay with John," said Mrs. Boyd. "She's devoted to us."

"Guess she'd rather stay with me than freeze," said the Indian.

"Will you promise to come back to the island tomorrow and search till you find her?"

"Oh, I'll find her," said Nanabush, in his comforting, sly voice. "We ought to be gettin' on now, if you folks want to be home before dark."

"Pat! Pat! Oh, where is Pat gone?" cried the young girls.

Pat came bounding out of the woods, rushed at the launch, scrambled on board, and sat there grinning.

"He's got some sense, anyhow," said the Indian.

"Sound the whistle, John," said Mrs. Boyd. "That might fetch her."

"What if she's dead!" cried the younger girl.

"You can't kill a cat," said Nanabush. He stretched out his dark hand and blew the whistle.

All eyes were turned to the woods.

The cook said, "I left a bowl of bread and milk for her, by the back door."

"Come, Mother," said Mr. Boyd, "it's no use. We can't wait any longer."

The launch looked like a toy boat as it moved among the islands. The reflection of the islands lay on the dark

160

blue lake, more perfect than the reality. They were deserted.

It was only an hour later when Harriet came back. She was tired and hungry, for she had been on a more strenuous hunt than usual. She had cut one of her feet, and the hunt had been unsuccessful. She had curled up in the hollow of a tree and slept long, on the far side of the island. She had heard faint shouts for her, but feline perversity had made her curl herself closer.

Now she circled the cottage, meowed outside the doors, leaped to the windowsills, and peered into the rooms. There was a desolate air about them. She went to the wharf and saw that the launch was not there. The family would return in the launch.

She glided back to the cottage and found the bowl of bread and milk. She attacked it greedily, but after a few mouthfuls her appetite left her. She began to wash her face, then to lick her coat to cleanliness and luster. Her coat was a pleasing combination of tawny yellow and brown. She had a hard, shrewd face, but there was affection in her.

The October sun sank in spectacular grandeur among the islands. There was no twilight. A blue, cold evening took possession. A few glittering stars were reflected in the lake. The air became bitterly cold, and a white, furry frost rimed the grass. Harriet crept into the canoe where Mrs. Boyd had lifted the canvas. There was a cushion in it. She curled herself up and slept.

At sunrise she leaped from the canoe and ran to the kitchen window. From its ledge she peered into the room. There was no fire. There was no cook. Harriet gave a faint meow of disappointment. She bent her acute sense of hearing to catch a sound of life in the cottage. All she heard was the whisper of little waves against the shore. Pointed leaves from the silver birches drifted in the golden air. It was very cold.

Harriet went to the bowl of bread and milk and began to eat it. She discovered that she was ravenous. But there was so much of it that she had to take breath before she could finish it. Even in her repletion she muttered a meow of longing. She was four years old, and she had never been separated from the Boyds before. Her mother and her grandmother had belonged to the Boyds. She knew their movements and their life as she knew the pads of her own paw.

The bowl was emptied. As empty and hollow as the world in which she now found herself. Mechanically she began to wash her face, groom the fine hair behind her ears till it was erect as the pile of fine velvet. She stretched out her hind leg and swiftly licked the fur on the rim of her thigh. In this attitude it could be seen that she was with young. Her little teats showed rosy and fresh.

She heard a rustle in the fallen leaves and turned her green eyes defensively, fearfully, in that direction. A pair of porcupines stood staring at her, side by side, their quills upright, their yellow teeth showing in their trepidation. They had come to investigate the empty cottage.

Harriet gave a hissing scream at them, making her face as horrifying as she could. She stared with her back to the kitchen door, screaming and making faces. The porcupines turned and ambled away, pushing into a dense growth of junipers.

An acorn clattered across the roof of the cottage and fell close to Harriet. She stood up, wondering what was coming next. The chipmunk that had watched the departure yesterday now looked over the eave at her. He knew she could not get at him where he was, but he longed to retrieve his acorn. His neat striped head darted from side to side; his eyes questioned her. Her tail lashed its implacable answer. He put his little paw against the side of his face and settled down to watch her.

With a sudden leap she sprang toward the acorn, curved her paw about it, toyed with it. Beneath her fur her muscles flowed as she bent low over the acorn as though loving it, leaped back from it in disdain.

Paw to cheek, the chipmunk watched her.

Then, from all the empty world about her, her misery came to taunt her. She was alone, except for the helpless kittens that stirred inside her. She sank to her belly and gave a plaintive meow.

For a long while she lay with closed eyes. The chipmunk longed for his acorn. No other acorn could take its place. He kept elongating his neck to see into Harriet's face. She seemed oblivious of everything, but he was not deceived. Still he could not resist. He darted down the wall of the cottage, made a dash for the acorn, snatched it.

He almost succeeded. But his nearness electrified her. In a flowing curve she sprang at him. He dropped the acorn and turned himself into wind and blew back against the wall of the cottage. From the eaves he chattered at her. She stared out across the lake, ignoring him.

As the sun neared the tops of the pines she heard the delicate approach of a canoe. She ran to a point of rock and crouched there, among the junipers, watching.

It was John Nanabush come to look for her. The lake was very still, and the reflection of canoe and Indian lay

163

on the glassy water, in silent companionship. He dipped and raised his paddle, as though caressing the lake. He gave glittering diamonds to it from the tip of his paddle. He called, in his indifferent Indian voice, "Horriet! Horriet! You there?"

She crouched, staring at him. She watched him with acute but contemptuous interest.

"Horriet! Horriet!" The canoe moved on, out of sight, behind a tumble of rocks, but the Indian's voice still echoed dreamily.

She would not go with him! She would not go. Surely there was a mistake! If she ran very fast to the house, she would find the family there. Harriet ran, in swift undulations, up the rocky, shaggy steep to the cottage.

The chipmunk watched her approach from the eave, his little paws pressed together as though in prayer. But he reviled her shrilly.

She ran along the veranda and sprang to the sill of the kitchen window. Inside it was almost dark. There was no cook. The frying pan hung against the wall. She heard the chipmunk scampering across the roof, in haste to get a good view of her. She sat down on the sill and opened her mouth, but no sound came.

The chipmunk peered down at her, turning his striped head this way and that, quivering in his excitement. She lashed her tail, but she would not look up at him. She began to lick her sore paw.

The red of the sky turned to a clear lemon color. There was an exquisite stillness, as the trees awaited the first hard frost. An icy fear, a terrible loneliness, descended on Harriet. She would not spend another night on the island.

The Ninth Life

As she ran to the water's edge she meowed without ceasing, as in protest against what she must do. A wedge-shaped flock of wild geese flew strong and sure against the yellow sky.

Before her the lake stretched dark blue, crisping in its coldness, lapping icily at her paws. She cried loudly in her protest as she walked into it. A few steps and she was out of her depth.

She had never swum before, but she could do so. She moved her paws knowingly, treading the icy water in fear and hate. A loon skimming the lake was startled by her stark cat's head rising out of the water and swung away, uttering his loud, wild laugh.

The next island was half a mile away. The last sunlight was held in the topmost branches of its pines. It seemed almost unattainable to Harriet, swimming in bitter stubbornness toward it. Sometimes she felt that she was sinking. The chill all but reached her heart; still she struggled toward the blackness of the rocks.

At last the island loomed above her. She smelled the scents of the land. All her hate of the water and her longing for home tautened her muscles. She swam fiercely and, before she was quite exhausted, clambered up on the rocks.

Once there, she was done. She lay flattened, a bit of wet draggled fur. But her heaving sides and gasping mouth showed that life was in her. The wet hairs of her fur began to crisp whitely in the frost. Her tail began to look stiff and brittle. She felt the spirit going out of her and the bitter cold coming in. The red afterglow on the black horizon was fading. It would soon be dark.

Harriet had a curious feeling of life somewhere near. Not

165

stirring, just sending its prickly essence in a thin current toward her. Her eyes flew open in horror of being attacked in her weak state. She looked straight into the eyes of a wild goose, spread on the rock near her.

One of his wings had been injured, and he had been left behind by the flock to die. He was large and strong, but young. This had been his first flight southward. His injured wing lay spread on the rock like a fan. He rested his glossy head on it.

They stared at each other, fascinated, while the current of his fear pricked her to life. She tightened the muscles of her belly and pressed her claws against the rock. Their eyes communed, each to each, like instruments in tune. She drew her chin against her frosty breast, while her eyes became balls of fire, glaring into his.

He raised himself above his broken wing and reared his strong other wing, as though to fly. But she held him with her eyes. He opened his long beak, but the cry died in his throat. He got onto his webbed feet and stood, with trailing wing, facing her. He moved a step nearer.

So they stared and stared till he wanted her to take him. He had no will but hers. Now her blood was moving quickly. She felt strong and fierce. His long neck, his big downy breast, were defenseless. She sprang, sunk her teeth in his neck, tore his breast with her hind claws, clung to him. His strong wing beat the air, even after he knew himself dying.

It was dark when she had finished her meal. She sat on the rock, washing her face, attending to her sore paw. The air had grown even colder, and snowflakes drifted on the darkness. The water in pools and shallows began to freeze.

166

The Ninth Life

Harriet crept close to the body of the goose, snuggling warmly in its down. She pressed under its wing, which spread above her, as though in protection.

She meowed plaintively as she prowled about the island next morning. The people who owned it had gone to their home, in a distant American city, many weeks ago. The windows of the cottage were boarded up. The flagstaff, where the big American flag had floated, was bare. Harriet prowled about the island, looking longingly at the mainland, filled with loathing of the icy water.

As she crept to its frozen rim she lifted her lip in loathing. A bit of down from the goose clung to her cheek. She crept onto the thin ice, and as it crackled beneath her she meowed as in pain. At last, with a despairing lash of her tail, she went into the lake and set her face toward the mainland. It was three quarters of a mile away.

This ordeal was worse than last night's. The lake was more cruelly cold. But it was smooth, stretched like cold steel beneath the drifting snowflakes. Harriet's four paws went up and down, as though the lake were a great barrier of ice she was mounting. Her head looked small and sleek as a rat's. Her green eyes were unwinking. Like a lodestone, the house at the foot of the lake drew her. Her spirit drew courage from the fire of its hearth.

A snake also was swimming to the mainland. Its cold blood felt no chill. Its ebony head arched above the steel of the lake. A delicate flourish on the steely surface followed it. The two swimmers were acutely conscious of each other's presence, but their cold eyes ignored it.

Harriet scrambled onto the crackling ice at the shore and lay prone. The life was all but gone from her. She remembered neither food nor fire nor shelter. The snake glided over the stones near her, slippery and secure. She tried to rise but could not.

The flurry of snow passed. A wind from the southwest made a scatteration among the clouds. They moved north and east, settling in gray and purple on the horizon. The sun shone out strongly, turning the October foliage to a blaze of scarlet and gold. The sunlight lay warm on Harriet's sagging sides.

She felt new life creeping into her. She raised her head and began to lick her sore paw. Then she ran her tongue, in long, eager strokes, across her flanks. Her fur stood upright. Her flesh grew warm and supple.

She crept out on a rock, from whose crevices hardy ferns and huckleberry bushes grew. A few huckleberries glimmered frostily blue among the russet leaves. Harriet peered into the pool below the rock. She saw some small bass resting there in the watered sunshine.

She crouched, watching them intently. Her colors mingled with the frost-browned fern and bronzed leaves. She settled herself on her breast, as though to rest, then her paws shot into the pool, her claws like fishhooks drove into the bright scales. The bass lay on the rock, its golden eye staring up at her.

Now she felt refreshed and strong. She found the sandy track through the woods and trotted along it toward the foot of the lake. All day she pressed forward, meeting no one. She stopped only to catch a little mouse and eat it and rest after the meal.

At sundown a deer stepped out of a thicket and stood before her, his antlers arching like the branches of a tree, his great eyes glowing. He looked at her, then bent his antlers, listening. He raised a shapely hoof and stood poised. Harriet saw something shining among the leaves. There was a sharp noise. The shock of it lifted Harriet from her feet, made every hair of her tail vibrant.

The tall deer sank to his knees. He laid the side of his head on the ground, and his great eyes were raised imploringly to the face of the hunter who came out of the wood. The hunter knelt by him, as though in compassion. Then a stream of red gushed from the deer's throat. A dog came and sniffed his flank. Harriet peered down from a tree where she had hid. It was long before she dared to go on.

She had gone only a short way when she saw a doe and a fawn, standing as though waiting. The doe lowered her head at Harriet, but the fawn looked proudly aloof, holding its head, with the face innocent as a little child's, high on its strong neck. Harriet glided away, her paws brushing the snow from the dead leaves. She curled herself in a hollow in a tree and lay licking her sore paw. She thought of the dead deer's great body and the large pieces of flesh she had seen cut from it.

In the morning she was very hungry, but there was nothing to eat. The sky was dark; the snow had turned to a rain that dripped from the trees and soaked her fur till it clung to her. But she ran steadily along the track, always drawn by the lodestone of the house at the foot of the lake. Passing toward it, she sometimes gave a meow as faint and thin as the fall of a pine needle. She ate a few blueberries from the dried bushes. She came to a space carpeted by glossy wintergreen leaves. She even ate some of the scarlet berries, eating them with distaste and curling lip, but she was very hungry because of the kittens she carried. There seemed nothing living abroad except her.

The path crossed a swamp dense with a growth of cranberries. Beyond it she came to a settler's cottage, clean and neat, with poultry in a wire run. There was a hen turkey in the yard, followed by three daintily moving poults. A girl was milking a cow in an open shed. Harriet stood staring, lonely, hungry. She felt weighted down, almost too tired to go on.

A man came out of the house with a bucket. He saw her, and a piercing whistle brought two hounds. He picked up a stone and threw it. It struck her side.

Harriet turned into a fury, an elongated, arched, fiery-eyed, sneering fury. The hounds hesitated before her claws that reached for their eyes. She whirled and flew down the path. They came after her, baying, sending up the volume of their voices in the rain. They urged each other on with loud cries. With her last strength she clambered into a tree and sat sneering down at them, her sides palpitating.

The hounds stood with their paws against the trunk of the tree, baying up at her. They changed places, as though that would help them. They flung themselves down, panting beneath the tree, then sprang up again, baying. But when the shrill whistle sounded again, they ran without hesitating back to their master.

On and on Harriet limped over the rock track. Sometimes she had a glimpse of the lake between trees, but she scarcely looked to right or left. The homeward cord drew her ever more strongly. One would scarcely have recognized the sleek pet in this draggled tramp, this limping, heavy-eyed, slinking cat.

The Ninth Life

She could see the twinkling lights of the town across the bay, when her pain came on. It was so piercing, so sudden, that she turned, with a savage cry, to face what seemed to be attacking her in the rear. But then she knew that the pain was inside her.

She lay writhing on the ground and before long gave birth to a kitten. She began to lick it, then realized that it was dead. She ran on toward the town as fast as she could.

She was still two miles from it when she had two more kittens. She lay beside them for a while, feeling weak and peaceful. Now the lights of the town were out. Harriet picked up one of the kittens and limped on. With it in her mouth she went along the paved street. She gave a meow of delight as she reached the back door of her own home.

She laid the kitten on the doorstep and herself began limping back and forth, the length of the step, rubbing her sides against the door. For the first time since she had been left on the island she purred. The purr bubbled in her throat, vibrating through her nerves in an ecstasy of homecoming. She caressed the back door with every bit of her. She stood on her hind legs and caressed the door handle with a loving paw. Only the weak cry of her kitten made her desist.

She carried it to the tool shed and laid it on the mat where the terrier slept in warm weather. She laid herself down beside it, trilling to it in love. It buried its sightless face against her lank belly. She lay flat on her side, weary to the bone.

But the shape of the kitten she had abandoned on the road now crept into her mind. It crept on silken paws, with its tail pointed like a rat's and its eyelids glued together.

Round and round it crept in its agony of abandonment, tearing her mind as its birth had torn her body. She flung herself on her other side, trying to forget it, but she could not.

With a piteous meow of protest against the instinct that hounded her, she left the kitten's side and went out into the dawn. The rain had stopped, and there was a sharp clear wind that drove the dead leaves scurrying across the frozen ruts.

The pain of her sore paw on the ice ruts was like fire, but she hurried on, draggled, hard-faced, with the thought of the bereft kitten prodding her.

The dreadful road unrolled itself before her in an endless scroll of horrible hieroglyphics. She meowed in hate of it, at every yard. She covered it, mile after mile, till she reached the spot where she had littered. There in the coarse, wet grass, she found the kitten. She turned it over with her nose, sniffing it to see if it were worth taking home. She decided that it was.

Along the road she limped, the kitten dangling from her unloving mouth, the dead leaves whirling about her, as though they would bury her, the icy ruts biting her paw.

But the clouds had broken, and the Indian-summer sun was leaping out. As she hobbled into her own yard her fur was warm and dry on her back. She laid the kitten beside the other and gave herself up to suckling them. And as they drew life from her, her love went out to them. She made soft trilling noises to them, threw her forelegs about them, lashed her tail about them, binding them close. She licked their fat bodies and their blunt heads till they shone.

Then suddenly a noise in the kitchen galvanized her.

The Ninth Life

She leaped up, scattering the sucklings from her nipples. It was the rattle of a stove lid she had heard. She ran up the steps and meowed at the back door. It opened, and the cook let out a scream of joy.

"Harriet! Harriet! Harriet's here!"

Pat ran to meet her, putting his paw on her back. She arched herself at him, giving a three-cornered smile. The cook ran to room after room, telling the news. The Boyds came from room after room to welcome Harriet, to marvel at her return.

"She must have come early last night," said the cook, "for she's had kittens in the tool shed."

"Well, they'll have to be drowned," said Mr. Boyd.

Harriet could not eat her bread and milk for purring. The purring sang in her throat, like a kettle. She had left her saucer and went to Mr. Boyd and thrust her head into his hand.

"Just listen how she purrs!" said Mrs. Boyd. "I've always said she was an affectionate cat."

The Cyprian Cat

DOROTHY L. SAYERS

It's extraordinarily decent of you to come along and see me like this, Harringay. Believe me, I do appreciate it. It isn't every busy K.C. who'd do as much for such a hopeless sort of client. I only 'wish I could spin you a more workable kind of story, but honestly I can only tell you exactly what I told Peabody. Of course, I can see he doesn't believe a word of it, and I don't blame him. He thinks I ought to be able to make up a more plausible tale than that, and I suppose I could, but where's the use? One's almost bound to fall down somewhere if one tries to

174

swear to a lie. What I'm going to tell you is the absolute truth. I fired one shot and one shot only, and that was at the cat. It's funny that one should be hanged for shooting at a cat.

Merridew and I were always the best of friends, school and college and all that sort of thing. We didn't see very much of each other after the war, because we were living at opposite ends of the country; but we met in town from time to time and wrote occasionally, and each of us knew that the other was there in the background, so to speak. Two years ago he wrote and told me he was getting married. He was just turned forty and the girl was fifteen years younger, and he was tremendously in love. It gave me a bit of a jolt. You know how it is when your friends marry. You feel they will never be quite the same again, and I'd got used to the idea that Merridew and I were cut out to be old bachelors. But of course I congratulated him and sent him a wedding present, and I did sincerely hope he'd be happy. He was obviously over head and ears, almost dangerously so, I thought, considering all things. Though except for the difference of age, it seemed suitable enough. He told me he had met her at—of all places—a rectory garden party down in Norfolk, and that she had actually never been out of her native village. I mean literally—not so much as a trip to the nearest town. I'm not trying to convey that she wasn't pukka, or anything like that. Her father was some queer sort of recluse—a medievalist or something—desperately poor. He died shortly after their marriage.

I didn't see anything of them for the first year or so. Merridew is a civil engineer, you know, and he took his wife away after the honeymoon to Liverpool, where he was doing something in connection with the harbor. It must have been a big change for her from the wilds of Norfolk. I was in Birmingham, with my nose kept pretty close to the grindstone, so we only exchanged occasional letters. His were what I can only call deliriously happy, especially at first. Later on, he seemed a little worried about his wife's health. She was restless; town life didn't suit her; he'd be glad when he could finish up his Liverpool job and get her away into the country. There wasn't any doubt about their happiness, you understand. She'd got him body and soul as they say, and as far as I could make out it was mutual. I want to make that perfectly clear.

Well, to cut a long story short, Merridew wrote to me at the beginning of last month and said he was just off to a new job, a waterworks extension scheme down in Somerset, and he asked if I could possibly cut loose and join them there for a few weeks. He wanted to have a yarn with me, and Felice was longing to make my acquaintance. They had got rooms at the village inn. It was rather a remote spot, but there was fishing and scenery and so forth, and I should be able to keep Felice company while he was working up at the dam. I was about fed up with Birmingham, what with the heat and one thing and another, and it looked pretty good to me, and I was due for a holiday anyhow, so I fixed up to go. I had a bit of business to do in town, which I calculated would take me about a week, so I said I'd go down to Little Hexham on June twentieth.

As it happened, my business in London finished itself

off unexpectedly soon, and on the sixteenth I found myself absolutely free and stuck in a hotel with road drills working just under the windows and a tar-spraying machine to make things livelier. You remember what a hot month it was—flaming June and no mistake about it. I didn't see any point in waiting, so I sent off a wire to Merridew, packed my bag, and took the train for Somerset the same evening. I couldn't get a compartment to myself, but I found a first-class smoker with only three seats occupied and stowed myself thankfully into the fourth corner. There was a military-looking old boy, an elderly female with a lot of bags and baskets, and a girl. I thought I should have a nice, peaceful journey.

So I should have, if it hadn't been for the unfortunate way I'm built. It was quite all right at first. As a matter of fact, I think I was half asleep, and I only woke up properly at seven o'clock, when the waiter came to say that dinner was on. The other people weren't taking it, and when I came back from the restaurant car I found that the old boy had gone, and there were only the two women left. I settled down in my corner again, and gradually, as we went along, I found a horrible feeling creeping over me that there was a cat in the compartment somewhere. I'm one of those wretched people who can't stand cats. I don't mean just that I prefer dogs. I mean that the presence of a cat in the same room with me makes me feel like nothing on earth. I can't describe it, but I believe quite a lot of people are affected that way. Something to do with electricity, or so they tell me. I've read that very often the dislike is mutual, but it isn't so with me. The brutes seem to find me abominably fascinating, make a beeline for my

177

legs every time. It's a funny sort of complaint, and it doesn't make me at all popular with dear old ladies.

Anyway, I began to feel more and more awful, and I realized that the old girl at the other end of the seat must have a cat in one of her innumerable baskets. I thought of asking her to put it out in the corridor or calling the guard and having it removed, but I knew how silly it would sound and made up my mind to try and stick it. I couldn't say the animal was misbehaving itself or anything, and she looked a pleasant old lady; it wasn't her fault that I was a freak. I tried to distract my mind by looking at the girl.

She was worth looking at, too—very slim and dark with one of those dead-white skins that make you think of magnolia blossom. She had the most astonishing eyes, too —I've never seen eyes quite like them—a very pale brown, almost amber, set wide apart and a little slanting, and they seemed to have a kind of luminosity of their own, if you get what I mean. I don't know if this sounds— I don't want you to think I was bowled over or anything. As a matter of fact, she held no sort of attraction for me, though I could imagine a different type of man going potty about her. She was just unusual, that was all. But however much I tried to think of other things I couldn't get rid of the uncomfortable feeling, and eventually I gave it up and went out into the corridor. I just mention this because it will help you to understand the rest of the story. If you can only realize how perfectly awful I feel when there's a cat about—even when it's shut up in a basket—you'll understand better how I came to buy the revolver.

Well, we got to Hexham Junction, which was the near-

178

est station to Little Hexham, and there was old Merridew waiting on the platform. The girl was getting out too—but not the old lady with the cat, thank goodness—and I was just handing her traps out after her when he came galloping up and hailed us.

"Hullo," he said, "why that's splendid! Have you introduced yourselves?" So I tumbled to it then that the girl was Mrs. Merridew, who'd been up to Town on a shopping expedition, and I explained to her about my change of plans, and she said how jolly it was that I could come—the usual things. I noticed what an attractive low voice she had and how graceful her movements were, and I understood—though, mind you, I didn't share—Merridew's infatuation.

We got into his car; Mrs. Merridew sat in the back, and I got up beside Merridew and was very glad to feel the air and to get rid of the oppressive electric feeling I'd had in the train. He told me the place suited them wonderfully and had given Felice an absolutely new lease on life, so to speak. He said he was very fit, too, but I thought myself that he looked rather fagged and nervy.

You'd have liked that inn, Harringay. The real, old-fashioned stuff, as quaint as you make 'em, and everything genuine—none of your Tottenham Court Road antiques. We'd all had our grub, and Mrs. Merridew said she was tired; so she went up to bed early, and Merridew and I had a drink and went for a stroll around the village. It's a tiny hamlet quite at the other end of nowhere; lights out at ten, little thatched houses with pinched-up attic windows like furry ears. The place purred in its sleep. Merridew's working gang didn't sleep there, of course; they'd put

179

up huts for them at the dams, a mile beyond the village.

The landlord was just locking up the bar when we came in, a block of a man with an absolutely expressionless face. His wife was a thin, sandy-haired woman who looked as though she was too downtrodden to open her mouth. But I found out afterward that was a mistake, for one evening when he'd taken one or two over the eight and showed signs of wanting to make a night of it, his wife sent him off upstairs with a gesture and a look that took the heart out of him. That first night she was sitting on the porch and hardly glanced at us as we passed her. I always thought her an uncomfortable kind of woman, but she certainly kept her house most exquisitely neat and clean.

They'd given me a noble bedroom, close under the eaves with a long, low casement window overlooking the garden. The sheets smelled of lavender, and I was between them and asleep almost before you could count ten. I was tired, you see. But later in the night I woke up. I was too hot, so took off some of the blankets and then strolled across to the window to get a breath of air. The garden was bathed in moonshine, and on the lawn I could see something twisting and turning oddly. I stared a bit before I made it out to be two cats. They didn't worry me at that distance, and I watched them for a bit before I turned in again. They were rolling over one another and jumping away again and chasing their own shadows on the grass, intent on their own mysterious business, taking themselves seriously, the way cats always do. It looked like a kind of ritual dance. Then something seemed to startle them, and they scampered away.

I went back to bed, but I couldn't get to sleep again.

The Cyprian Cat

My nerves seemed to be all on edge. I lay watching the window and listening to a kind of soft rustling noise that seemed to be going on in the big wisteria that ran along my side of the house. And then something landed with a soft thud on the sill—a great Cyprian cat.

What did you say? Well, one of those striped gray-and-black cats. Tabby, that's right. In my part of the country they call them Cyprus cats, or Cyprian cats. I'd never seen such a monster. It stood with its head cocked sideways, staring into the room and rubbing its ears very softly against the upright bar of the casement.

Of course, I couldn't do with that. I shooed the brute away, and it made off without a sound. Heat or no heat, I shut and fastened the window. Far out in the shrubbery I thought I heard a faint miauling, then silence. After that, I went straight off to sleep again and lay like a log till the girl came in to call me.

The next day Merridew ran us up in his car to see the place where they were making the dam, and that was the first time I realized that Felice's nerviness had not been altogether cured. He showed us where they had diverted part of the river into a swift little stream that was to be used for working the dynamo of an electrical plant. There were a couple of planks laid across the stream, and he wanted to take us over to show us the engine. It wasn't extraordinarily wide or dangerous, but Mrs. Merridew peremptorily refused to cross it and got quite hysterical when he tried to insist. Eventually he and I went over and inspected the machinery by ourselves. When we got back, she had recovered her temper and apologized for being so silly. Merridew abased himself, of course, and I

181

began to feel a little *de trop*. She told me afterward that she had once fallen into the river as a child and been nearly drowned, and it had left her with a what d'ye call it—a complex about running water. And but for this one trifling episode, I never heard a single sharp word pass between them all the time I was there; nor, for a whole week, did I notice anything else to suggest a flaw in Mrs. Merridew's radiant health. Indeed, as the days wore on to midsummer and the heat grew more intense, her whole body seemed to glow with vitality. It was as though she was lit up from within.

Merridew was out all day and working very hard. I thought he was overdoing it and asked him if he was sleeping badly. He told me that, on the contrary, he fell asleep every night the moment his head touched the pillow and—what was most unusual with him—had no dreams of any kind. I myself felt well enough, but the hot weather made me languid and disinclined for exertion. Mrs. Merridew took me out for long drives in the car. I would sit for hours, lulled into a half slumber by the rush of warm air and the purring of the engine and gazing at my driver, upright at the wheel, her eyes fixed unwaveringly upon the spinning road. We explored the whole of the country to the south and east of Little Hexham, and once or twice went as far north as Bath. Once I suggested that we should turn eastward over the bridge and run down into what looked like rather beautiful wooded country, but Mrs. Merridew didn't care for the idea; she said it was a bad road and that the scenery on that side was disappointing.

Altogether I spent a pleasant week at Little Hexham, and if it had not been for the cats I should have been perfectly comfortable. Every night the garden seemed to be haunted by them—the Cyprian cat that I had seen the first night of my stay, a little ginger one, and a horrible stinking black Tom were especially tiresome. And one night there was a terrified white kitten that mewed for an hour on end under my window. I flung boots and books at my visitors till I was heartily weary, but they seemed determined to make the inn garden their rendezvous. The nuisance grew worse from night to night; on one occasion I counted fifteen of them, sitting on their hinder ends in a circle, while the Cyprian cat danced her shadow dance among them, working in and out like a weaver's shuttle. I had to keep my window shut, for the Cyprian cat evidently made a habit of climbing up by the wisteria. The door, too, for once when I had gone down to fetch something from the sitting room, I found her on my bed, kneading the coverlet with her paws—*pr'rp, pr'rp, pr'rp*—with her eyes closed in a sensuous ecstasy. I beat her off, and she spat at me as she fled into the dark passage.

I asked the landlady about her, but she replied rather curtly that they kept no cat at the inn, and it is true that I never saw any of the beasts in the daytime. One evening, however, about dusk I caught the landlord in one of the outhouses. He had the ginger cat on his shoulder and was feeding her with something that looked like strips of liver. I remonstrated with him for encouraging the cats about the place and asked whether I could have a different room, explaining that the nightly caterwauling disturbed me. He half opened his slits of eyes and murmured that he would ask his wife about it, but nothing was done, and in fact I believe there was no other bedroom in the house.

183

And all this time the weather got hotter and heavier, working up for thunder, with the sky like brass and the earth like iron, and the air quivering over it so that it hurt your eyes to look at it.

All right, Harringay, I am trying to keep to the point. And I'm not concealing anything from you. I say that my relations with Mrs. Merridew were perfectly ordinary. Of course, I saw a good deal of her, because as I explained Merridew was out all day. We went up to the dam with him in the morning and brought the car back, and naturally we had to amuse one another as best we could till the evening. She seemed quite pleased to be in my company, and I couldn't dislike her. I can't tell you what we talked about—nothing in particular. She was not a talkative woman. She would sit or lie for hours in the sunshine, hardly speaking, only stretching out her body to the light and heat. Sometimes she would spend a whole afternoon playing with a twig or a pebble, while I sat and smoked. Restful! No. No, I shouldn't call her a restful personality exactly. Not to me, at any rate. In the evening she would liven up and talk a little more, but she generally went up to bed early and left Merridew and me to yarn together in the garden.

Oh, about the revolver! Yes. I bought that in Bath, when I had been at Little Hexham exactly a week. We drove over in the morning, and while Mrs. Merridew got some things for her husband, I prowled around the secondhand shops. I had intended to get an air gun or a peashooter or something of that kind, when I saw this. You've seen it, of course. It's very tiny—what people in books describe as "little more than a toy"—but deadly enough. The old boy who sold it to me didn't seem to know much about fire-arms. He'd taken it in pawn sometime back, he told me, and there were ten rounds of ammunition with it. He made no bones about a license or anything, glad enough to make a sale, no doubt, without putting difficulties in a customer's way. I told him I knew how to handle it and mentioned by way of a joke that I meant to take a potshot or two at the cats. That seemed to wake him up a bit. He was a dried-up little fellow, with a scrawny gray beard and a stringy neck. He asked me where I was staying. I told him at Little Hexham.

"You better be careful, sir," he said. "They think a heap of their cats down there, and it's reckoned unlucky to kill them." And then he added something I couldn't quite catch, about a silver bullet. He was a doddering old fellow, and he seemed to have some sort of scruple about letting me take the parcel away, but I assured him that I was perfectly capable of looking after it and myself. I left him standing in the door of his shop, pulling at his beard and staring after me.

That night the thunder came. The sky had turned to lead before evening, but the dull heat was more oppressive than the sunshine. Both the Merridews seemed to be in a state of nerves—he sulky and swearing at the weather and the flies, and she wrought up to a queer kind of vivid excite-ment. Thunder affects some people that way. I wasn't much better, and to make things worse I got the feeling that the house was full of cats. I couldn't see them, but I knew they were there, lurking behind the cupboards and flitting noiselessly about the corridors. I could scarcely sit in the parlor and was thankful to escape to my room.

Cats or no cats I had to open the window, and I sat there with my pajama jacket unbuttoned, trying to get a breath of air. But the place was like the inside of a copper furnace. And pitch-dark. I could scarcely see from my window where the bushes ended and the lawn began. But I could hear and feel the cats. There were little scrapings in the wisteria and scufflings among the leaves, and about eleven o'clock one of them started the concert with a loud and hideous wail. Then another and another joined in—I'll swear there were fifty of them. And presently I got that foul sensation of nausea, and the flesh crawled on my bones, and I knew that one of them was slinking close to me in the darkness.

I looked around quickly, and there she stood, the great Cyprian, right against my shoulder, her eyes glowing like green lamps. I yelled and struck out at her, and she snarled as she leaped out and down. I heard her thump the gravel, and the yowling burst out all over the garden with renewed vehemence. And then all in a moment there was utter silence, and in the far distance there came a flickering blue flash and then another. In the first of them I saw the far garden wall, topped along all its length with cats, like a nursery frieze. When the second flash came the wall was empty.

At two o'clock the rain came. For three hours before that I had sat there, watching the lightning as it spat across the sky and exulting in the crash of the thunder. The storm seemed to carry off all the electrical disturbance in my body; I could have shouted with excitement and relief. Then the first heavy drops fell, then a steady downpour, then a deluge. It struck the iron-baked garden with a noise

186

like steel rods falling. The smell of the ground came up intoxicatingly, and the wind rose and flung the rain in against my face. At the other end of the passage I heard a window thrown to and fastened, but I leaned out into the tumult and let the water drench my head and shoulders. The thunder still rumbled intermittently, but with less noise and farther off, and in an occasional flash I saw the white grille of falling water drawn between me and the garden.

It was after one of these thunderpeals that I became aware of a knocking at my door. I opened it, and there was Merridew. He had a candle in his hand, and his face was terrified.

"Felice!" he said abruptly. "She's ill. I can't wake her. For God's sake, come and give me a hand."

I hurried down the passage after him. There were two beds in his room—a great four-poster, hung with crimson damask, and a small camp bedstead drawn up near to the window. The small bed was empty, the bedclothes tossed aside; evidently he had just risen from it. In the four-poster lay Mrs. Merridew, naked, with only a sheet upon her. She was stretched flat upon her back, her long black hair in two plaits over her shoulders. Her face was waxen and shrunk, like the face of a corpse, and her pulse, when I felt it, was so faint that at first I could scarcely feel it. Her breathing was very slow and shallow and her flesh cold. I shook her, but there was no response at all. I lifted her eyelids and noticed how the eyeballs were turned up under the upper lid, so that only the whites were visible. The touch of my fingertip upon the sensitive ball evoked no reaction. I immediately wondered whether she took drugs.

Merridew seemed to think it necessary to make some explanation. He was babbling about the heat—she couldn't bear so much as a silk nightgown—she had suggested that he should occupy the other bed—he had slept heavily—right through the thunder. The rain blowing in on his face had aroused him. He had got up and shut the window. Then he had called to Felice to know if she was all right; he thought the storm might have frightened her. There was no answer. He had struck a light. Her condition had alarmed him, and so on.

I told him to pull himself together and to try whether, by chafing his wife's hands and feet, we could restore the circulation. I had it firmly in my mind that she was under the influence of some opiate. We set to work, rubbing and pinching and slapping her with wet towels and shouting her name in her ear. It was like handling a dead woman, except for the very slight but perfectly regular rise and fall of her bosom, on which—with a kind of surprise that there should be any flaw on its magnolia whiteness—I noticed a large brown mole, just over the heart. To my perturbed fancy it suggested a wound and a menace. We had been at it for some time, with the sweat pouring off us, when we became aware of something going on outside the window—a stealthy bumping and scraping against the panes. I snatched up the candle and looked out.

On the sill, the Cyprian cat sat and clawed at the casement. Her drenched fur clung limply to her body; her eyes glared into mine; her mouth was opened in protest. She scrabbled furiously at the latch, her hind claws slipping and scratching on the woodwork. I hammered on the pane and bawled at her, and she struck back at the glass as though possessed. As I cursed her and turned away she set up a long, despairing wail.

Merridew called to me to bring back the candle and leave the brute alone. I returned to the bed, but the dismal crying went on and on incessantly. I suggested to Merridew that he should wake the landlord and get hot-water bottles and some brandy from the bar and see if a messenger could not be sent for a doctor. He departed on this errand, while I went on with my massage. It seemed to me that the pulse was growing still fainter. Then I suddenly recollected that I had a small brandy flask in my bag. I ran out to fetch it, and as I did so the cat suddenly stopped its howling.

As I entered my own room the air blowing through the open window struck gratefully upon me. I found my bag in the dark and was rummaging for the flask among my shirts and socks when I heard a loud, triumphant mew and turned around in time to see the Cyprian cat crouched for a moment on the sill, before it sprang in past me and out at the door. I found the flask and hastened back with it, just as Merridew and the landlord came running up the stairs.

We all went into the room together. As we did so, Mrs. Merridew stirred, sat up, and asked us what in the world was the matter.

I have seldom felt quite such a fool.

Next day the weather was cooler; the storm had cleared the air. What Merridew had said to his wife I do not know. None of us made any public allusion to the night's disturbance, and to all appearance Mrs. Merridew was in the best of health and spirits. Merridew took a day off from the waterworks, and we all went for a long drive and picnic together. We were on the best of terms with one another. Ask Merridew. He will tell you the same thing. He would not—he could not, surely—say otherwise. I can't believe, Harringay, I simply cannot believe that he could imagine or suspect me. I say, there was nothing to suspect. Nothing.

Yes—this is the important date—the twenty-fourth of June. I can't tell you any more details; there is nothing to tell. We came back and had dinner just as usual. All three of us were together all day, till bedtime. On my honor I had no private interview of any kind that day, either with him or with her. I was the first to go to bed, and I heard the others come upstairs about half an hour later. They were talking cheerfully.

It was a moonlight night. For once, no caterwauling came to trouble me. I didn't even bother to shut the window or the door. I put the revolver on the chair beside me before I lay down. Yes, it was loaded. I had no special object in putting it there, except that I meant to have a go at the cats if they started their games again.

I was desperately tired and thought I should drop off to sleep at once, but I didn't. I must have been overtired, I suppose. I lay and looked at the moonlight. And then, about midnight, I heard what I had been half expecting: a stealthy scrabbling in the wisteria and a faint miauling sound.

I sat up in bed and reached for the revolver. I heard the *plop* as the big cat sprang up onto the window ledge; I saw her black and silver flanks and the outline of her round head, pricked ears, and upright tail. I aimed and fired, and the beast let out one frightful cry and sprang down into the room.

I jumped out of bed. The crack of the shot had sounded terrific in the silent house, and somewhere I heard a distant voice call out. I pursued the cat into the passage, revolver in hand, with some idea of finishing it off, I suppose. And then, at the door of the Merridews' room, I saw Mrs. Merridew. She stood with one hand on each doorpost, swaying to and fro. Then she fell down at my feet. Her bare breast was all stained with blood. And as I stood staring at her, clutching the revolver, Merridew came out and found us—like that.

Well, Harringay, that's my story, exactly as I told it to Peabody. I'm afraid it won't sound very well in Court, but what can I say? The trail of blood led from my room to hers; the cat must have run that way; I *know* it was the cat I shot. I can't offer any explanation. I don't know who shot Mrs. Merridew, or why. I can't help it if the people at the inn say they never saw the Cyprian cat; Merridew saw it that other night, and I know he wouldn't lie about it. Search the house, Harringay. That's the only thing to do. Pull the place to pieces, till you find the body of the Cyprian cat. It will have my bullet in it.

About the Editor

Phyllis R. Fenner was born in Almond, New York, and for thirty-two years was the librarian of the Plandome Road School in Manhasset, New York. In 1955, she retired and made her permanent home in Manchester, Vermont. She holds degrees from Mount Holyoke College and from the Columbia Library School, and she has traveled extensively throughout this country, Canada, Mexico, and Europe.

Miss Fenner's work has brought her in touch with library schools throughout the country; she has also done book reviewing, given lectures about children's books, and held story hours for children. In addition, she is widely known for her many distinguished anthologies.